76

ESCAPE INTO SPACE

Geldray, working for the government in building a starship, fears world destruction. So he privately plans to make the vessel a colonising project. Meanwhile, power-crazed Edward Smith intends to destroy all obstacles in his way — including Geldray, project Star and the politician Melgrath's reputation — in order to take over the government. Realising Smith's intentions, Geldray's last act is to launch the starship. Will the ship's crew succeed in escaping into space to find a new home amongst the stars?

E. C. TUBB

ESCAPE INTO SPACE

Complete and Unabridged

LINFORD
Leicester

First published in Great Britain

First Linford Edition
published 2009

British Library CIP Data

Tubb, E. C.
  Escape into space
  1. Science fiction.
  2. Large type books.
  I. Title
  823.9′14–dc22

  ISBN 978–1–84782–714–2

Published by
F. A. Thorpe (Publishing)
Anstey, Leicestershire

Set by Words & Graphics Ltd.
Anstey, Leicestershire
Printed and bound in Great Britain by
T. J. International Ltd., Padstow, Cornwall

This book is printed on acid-free paper

To
IRIS

1

They left at dawn, heading west and racing the sun, landing as the pale light bleached the stars from the sky. The pilot was young, relaxed. Melgrath, his lone passenger, was neither. He had sat tense and anxious during the two hours plus they had been in the air since leaving Washington. His circulation was bad, his legs prone to cramp. As he stepped from the cabin he stumbled and almost fell.

'Steady!' A field-guard caught his arm. 'Are you all right, sir?'

'I can manage.' He shrugged off the supporting hand and stood blinking in the clear, hard light of the desert. An old, tired, worried man. The product of too little sleep, too little exercise, too much energy spent in trying to do the impossible. 'My plane,' he said. 'I want it serviced for immediate flight.'

The guard nodded. 'And the pilot?'

Melgrath looked at the young man where he stood in the open door of the cabin. His head was thrown back, eyes narrowed against the sun as he stared at the buildings of the project, the sequoia-tall bulk of the ship. 'He's young,' he said. 'And probably hungry. Can you fix him something to eat?'

'We'll look after him,' said the guard. 'And you, sir?'

'Take me to Geldray.'

Early as it was the head of the project was up and waiting in his office. It was a big place, air-conditioned, littered with files and papers. A place in which to work, not a part of an impressive façade. One entire wall was of glass; the picture-window framing the heart of the project, the tremendous bulk of the ship.

Melgrath had seen it before, seen it when it had been nothing but a skeleton of metal-fabric and it seemed to him that, as the ship had grown, so Geldray had shrivelled. Like a fly, he thought. Caught in a web of his own making. Sucked dry by the monster he had created. It's taken his health, he told himself. His money.

Years of his life. It's cost his reputation and now it's going to take his freedom. What the hell made him do it?

'Jack.' Geldray came from behind his desk, hand outstretched. 'It's good to see you.' They touched hands. 'You look all in,' he said. 'You want something? Coffee? Breakfast?'

'No thanks,' said Melgrath. 'No time.'

'There's time.' Geldray moved to his desk, pressed a button. 'Bring coffee,' he ordered. 'For two.' He looked at his visitor. 'Something must be really hot for you to have come all the way out here. Couldn't you have phoned?'

'No,' said Melgrath flatly. 'Not with all the bugs there are about. I'm no coward but I've no intention of handing them my head on a platter.'

'As bad as that?'

'Worse. This is the end, Sam. Finish. The balloon's burst and it's every man for himself. I thought you should know.' It was a relief to have said it, to have delivered the bombshell. 'Get this straight,' he added as Geldray made no answer. 'Your head's on the block, Sam.

3

It's only a matter of time before you feel the axe.'

'Smith?'

'Who else?' Melgrath was bitter. 'The man's crazy. I've been in politics all my life but he's got me beat. No deals. No compromise. Nothing. He forced Congress to appoint him head of the investigation into government appropriations and expenditure. He heads the Citizens Corps and the votes they command. He preaches clean government and means it. He's dug up more dirt since he took office than any other twenty senators. He's a nut,' he added savagely. 'A nut!'

'I doubt it,' said Geldray. He fell silent as a girl brought in the coffee, continuing as she left. 'He's a fanatic,' he said. 'A dangerous man. But he knows what he's doing. Sugar?'

'Two lumps.' Melgrath took the cup and sipped at the strong, black coffee. It helped. 'He's after blood, Sam,' he said. 'The higher they come the better he likes it. You're his next target and he's got his finger on the trigger ready to shoot you

4

down.' He drank more coffee. 'And he can't miss,' he added. 'He knows and we know that. He's got you cold.'

'Maybe.' Geldray stared thoughtfully at the scene in the window. 'We've been through this before,' he said quietly. 'Can't it be fixed?'

'Not this time.' Melgrath was emphatic. 'That's what I'm telling you. I've spent ten days trying. It can't be done.'

'There are more ways than one of skinning a cat, Jack.'

'Assassination?'

Melgrath finished his coffee and set down the empty cup. 'I've thought about it,' he admitted. 'But even if you could get to him you can't stop what he stands for with a bullet. There are too many ready to take over. You've got to face it, Sam. This time the chickens have really come home to roost.'

'I need time,' said Geldray. 'Time!'

'You haven't got it,' Melgrath said bluntly. 'It's running out. And so am I.'

'You?'

'Sure, why not? I'm in this as deep as you are. If I stay around I'll be forced to

5

testify against you. I don't want to do that. I don't want to spend the rest of my life in jail either. So I'm heading south while I've got the chance.' Melgrath hesitated. 'Look,' he said. 'The plane will hold more than one and the pilot knows how to keep his mouth shut. How about coming with me?'

Geldray shook his head.

'Why not? The ship's built, isn't it? You've done what you set out to do. What's the point of waiting around for Smith's goons? Skip now while there's still time.'

'I can't do that.'

'No? What's stopping you? Money? I've enough salted away for the both of us. Hell,' added Melgrath generously, 'it was your money to start with. You're welcome to some of it back.'

Geldray shook his head; the man simply didn't understand. A professional lobbyist had to be long on gall and short on imagination. 'The job isn't finished yet,' he explained. 'It won't be finished until that ship is off the ground and into space.'

'Then you'd better get it moving,' said Melgrath. 'All Smith needs to do is to get an injunction, freeze the project and ground the ship.' He stepped to where Geldray was standing and looked past him at the bulk of the vessel. It shone in the light of the newly risen sun. 'You know,' he said sourly. 'That thing out there could be about the biggest headstone a man ever had.'

'Not a headstone,' corrected Geldray. 'A monument.'

'There's a difference?'

'Yes,' said Geldray softly. 'There's a hell of a difference.'

★　★　★

The boy wore olive green pants and blouse, jet black boots and belt. Interlinked C's shone on his collar. He dropped a sheaf of advertising layouts on the desk, took a step backward, saluted. 'The mock-ups for the new campaign, sir,' he said.

'All right,' said Edward Smith.

'Is there anything else, sir?'

'Not yet.' Smith flashed his famous smile. 'Back to the grindstone, son.'

'Yes, sir!' The boy saluted again, spun on his heel, marched from the office. Edward Smith watched him go, warmly conscious of his power, the influence he had over others. Give them a uniform, he thought. A slogan to live by. Something to fight against. Mix it with patriotism, xenophobia, a touch of envy. Give them companions. And, as the twig is bent, so grows the tree.

It's an old formula, he told himself. A simple, basic method of getting to the top and staying there. It had happened in other countries and it could happen right here. The Citizens Corps was growing all the time. Numbers meant the control of a significant vote. Votes meant power. And power, he reminded himself, could be made self-perpetuating. All it took was time and a little manipulation.

He picked up the sheaf of mock-ups, studied them, punched a button on his desk. 'Mary? Tell Harry to get in here. Fast.'

Smith was engrossed in the mock-ups

when Harry Tigue entered. He didn't look up until the other had plumped himself into a chair and lit a cigar. Then he said. 'This campaign, Harry. There's something wrong.'

'How so?' Harry was a trained adman who knew his job. He stood up, leaned on the desk, looked at the layouts. 'It's got punch, drive, impact and alliteration. CONSUMERS' CO-OPERATIVE! It fits, Ed. It ties in with the 2C motive — CITIZENS CORPS; CLEAN CONTROL; CONSISTENT CREDIBILITY. It's got bite.'

'Maybe.' Smith leaned back in his chair. 'You've done a good job, Harry, I'm not saying you haven't, but I don't like the word 'co-operative'. It's too much like 'collective'. Too Commie. We need something else. Something domestic.'

'Russia's respectable,' reminded Tigue. 'We've been allies since '71.'

'I know that. But we're not allies with China and they're Commie. The Congofederation too. Commie still means 'foreigner' to our people.' He paused, tilting his head, studying the ceiling. 'Combine,' he decided. 'We'll use the word 'combine'. It's sharper, has more power, less syllables. CONSUMERS' COMBINE,' he said. 'That's it.'

'I'll make the change,' said Harry.

'Get the stickers printed and ready for nation-wide distribution,' said Smith. 'Alert all area officers to sound out prospective supporters. No threats, mind. Just the hint that, if they hope to retain corps members as customers, they'd better display a sticker. Set the initial fee at one hundred dollars — a donation to campaign expenses.'

Tigue nodded. 'When do you think you'll be ready?'

'For the major push?' Smith lit a cigarette. 'Soon,' he said. 'Project Star will do it. I'll expose Geldray and prove the administration rotten with corruption. With that evidence I'll be able to impeach the President and force new elections. With the support already promised plus the backlash of public opinion we'll ride home on a landslide.'

Tigue looked doubtful. 'I'm not sure,' he said slowly. 'Don't underestimate the opposition. Project Star is still a government operation and a part of our outer space research programme.'

'That,' said Smith deliberately, 'is a lie.' He drew at his cigarette. 'It's a lie the public have been forced to swallow but it simply isn't the truth. Let's just take a look at the facts.' He reached for a folder on his desk, flipped the pages. 'Ten years ago Sam Geldray was rich, wifeless, childless, neutral in politics. Then, instead of buying himself a blonde and having fun in Florida, he got himself appointed head of Project Star.'

'I know that.'

'Did you know how he did it? Geldray is no scientist. He had no political affiliations. He had nothing but money. He used it to buy political power and then used that power to launch the project, keep it afloat and keep it solvent. The damn thing's cost billions! God alone knows how much it's really cost what with sub-contracts and the like. Project Star is nothing but an excuse for certain politicians and business men to indulge in a mammoth system of robbing the taxpayer!'

'Calm down,' said Tigue quietly.

11

'You're not making a speech.' He flipped the folder with the tip of one finger. 'Saying it is one thing,' he reminded. 'Proving it is another. Can you?'

'Prove it?' Smith nodded. 'I've got sworn testimony of undercover deals, bank statements, copies of contracts, the works. I've got witnesses. Geldray's out on a limb. All we have to do is saw it off and down comes the government.'

'Slow down,' said Tigue. He was frowning. 'I don't get this,' he mused. 'Geldray's no fool. How come he left himself so wide open?'

'He didn't,' admitted Smith. 'It took digging to find out the real facts. And get this. He met up with two other men at about the time he started laying the groundwork for the project. Jacques Michele and John Dolman. Michele's a French scientist and . . . '

'Not French,' interrupted Tigue. 'French-Canadian. There's a difference.'

'Forget it,' commented Smith. 'From now on he's French. A foreigner. A man paid by us to do important research. But a foreigner. Remember that.' Smith crushed out his cigarette. 'And Dolman? You know him too?'

Tigue shook his head.

'Ten years ago he was a laugh. Doctor 'Doom' Dolman; that's what the papers called him. He made frontpage news during the silly season. He claimed the world was in danger from the effects of released radiation from atomic tests and the like. Naturally, no one took him seriously.'

'Maybe they should have,' said Tigue thoughtfully. 'I could show you figures that backed him up.'

'Forget them.' Smith was impatient with his aide. 'Or rather use them against him. The buggy-whip gimmick,' he explained. 'In 1870 any statistician would have told you that, in fifty years, the demand for buggy-whips would be enormous. They based their figures on the population-growth. They didn't know that anyone would invent the automobile. The point is,' he added, 'it doesn't matter what Dolman believes. We have to make him out as a nut.'

'And Michele?'

'I'm not sure about him.' Smith frowned thoughtfully at the opposite wall. 'His qualifications are genuine. He could have something in that ship worth every cent poured into the project. But we'll keep that under wraps,' he said briskly. 'We simply want to prove that Geldray is a criminal who has stolen public money. That the administration either was too ignorant to know, or otherwise condoned what was going on. That the whole project is a stinking mass of bribery, graft and corruption. And,' he ended, 'that the safety of the nation has been imperilled by the utter lack of any form of recognized security.'

Tigue raised his eyebrows.

'It's true,' said Smith. 'No recognized branch of the government has anything to do with Project Star. The thing is a one-man band. I'll be damned if I know how Geldray managed it,' he admitted. 'But he did. And it helps to put his head on the block.'

'You're forgetting something,' reminded Tigue. He was a man who insisted on looking at both sides of every coin. 'Don't forget what the project is for. The public are suckers for romance.'

'Not this time,' said Smith with conviction. 'With a general shortage, a king-sized depression breathing down their necks and the sound of rattling sabres all over the world, what the hell do they care about reaching the stars? What good will it do them? What will they gain?'

'Nothing,' admitted Tigue. He puffed at his cigar. It had gone out and slowly he relit it. 'You know,' he said thoughtfully, 'there's one thing that bothers me. Geldray is no fool and yet he's left himself wide open. Now why should he have done that?'

'How should I know? Crazy, maybe?'

'Maybe,' agreed Tigue. 'Crazy — or scared.'

★ ★ ★

The tall, rangy Texan rolled lecherous eyes and his hands reached for the woman. Celia Forrest had been an army nurse adding M.D. after her name and

15

avoided the embrace with automatic skill. He tried again and she thrust a thermometer into his mouth. 'Sit down,' she ordered. 'I'll be with you in a minute. And keep that in,' she insisted as he tried to talk. 'The trouble with you roosters is that you don't know when to perch.'

She smiled as she said it and the Texan relaxed. In the inner office Doctor Dolman had noticed the exchange. He wasn't surprised. At thirty-two Celia was an attractive woman but that wasn't the answer.

They know, he thought. Deep inside, right down in the subconscious, they know. Nature has warned the race of its danger, he told himself. Something primeval is struggling for survival in the only way it knows how. By procreation. By an endless stream of young hoping that, somehow, a few might survive. Homo Sapiens, he thought. Turning to the habits of the rabbit. Filling every waking minute with the biological reflex of the courtship-dance.

He stepped into the office, nodded to the Texan, spoke to the woman. 'I'll take over, Doctor.'

'As you wish, Doctor.'

She stepped back as he approached the Texan. He removed the thermometer, glanced at it, dropped it into its receptacle. 'Just what seems to be the trouble?'

'Nothin' much,' drawled the Texan. 'It's jest that ah tires mighty fast. To what I used to,' he added. 'Cain't understand it. Ah eats well, drinks moderate, sleeps regular.'

'Where do you work?'

'On the pile. Ah trucks stuff to the ship. Ma work ain't suffered none,' he said quickly. Even on the project the spectre of unemployment had made itself felt. 'Ah does ma share.'

'I'm sure that you do.' Dolman stood, brooding, then went through the mechanical motions of examining the man. 'Have you ever felt like this before?'

'No.' The Texan was emphatic. 'Jest lately. A week or more is all. I figured that you could give me a little somethin',' he said. 'Ah guess that ah could use a tonic.'

'I'll give you something,' said Dolman.

One of the amphetamines to lift the inevitable depression, he thought. Coupled with a little cantharides to make what the man had left of life worth living. And it would keep him quiet; that was the important thing. 'Some of the purple tablets,' he said to the woman. 'You know where they are kept.'

'Yes, Doctor.' She met his eyes. 'How many?'

How much life could the man expect? A week? Two?

'Fifty,' he said, and waited until she had returned with the box: 'Here.' He handed it to the Texan. 'Take one each morning and another after work in the evening. Double the dose if you want to but don't take more than four a day. And stay out of the sun.'

'Sure, Doc,' said the Texan. 'Ah'll remember that. And thanks.'

Dolman felt the woman at his side as he watched the man walk across the desert away from the surgery. It was symbolic, he thought, that he had to pass through the shadow of the ship. 'The usual, John?'

'Yes,' he said, and then, savagely. 'What's the matter? Do you want me to spell it out for you? That man is dying from radiation poisoning caused by his work on the pile. He hasn't a hope in hell of lasting more than a few days. He's already dead — a walking, talking corpse.'

'The fifth in two days,' she reminded.

'There'll be more,' he said grimly. 'But it doesn't matter. The ship has to be loaded ready for flight. That's all that counts. If fifty men have to die to get it done then they have to die. Our job is to keep them quiet while they're doing it.' He turned to face her. 'Listen,' he said. 'You know what Geldray told us. We're racing against time. We can't afford to be squeamish. We've got to finish what we set out to do.'

'I know that,' she said. 'But do I have to like it?'

'You can do as you damn well please,' he snapped coldly. 'But do it. That's all.'

'Yes, Doctor.'

'Bitch,' he said without heat. 'Do you

think I like doing this?'

She shook her head.

'Would it matter so much if I did?' he demanded. Then, quickly. 'Don't answer that. It was a stupid question. Of course it would matter. You and I are doctors and it's our job to save life, not to act as dispensers of euthanasia. But sometimes the means justifies the end. We've got to remember that.'

'I know,' she said. 'I wasn't condemning you for anything.'

'No,' he said, and felt the sagging of his shoulders. 'I didn't think you were. You'd better get over to the ship,' he ordered. 'You'll be needed in the honeycomb. There's life there,' he added. 'You belong with the living. I'll handle the dead.'

'John,' she began. 'I — '

'Forget it,' he snapped. 'And get moving. We haven't all that much time.'

He watched her leave as he had watched the Texan but this time there was a difference. She's beautiful, he thought. More than that. Intelligent as well as attractive. I should have met a woman like her years ago, he told himself. Maybe then I wouldn't have felt so much alone — so damn guilty at thinking of her as other than a daughter. It's the syndrome, he reminded himself. Mother Nature's way of assuring the survival of the race. Why should I be immune?

He stepped from the surgery into the open desert. The air was crystal clear but, to him, it was filled with dirt and filth. Invisible filth. The residue of countless atomic tests as nation after nation flexed giant muscles in warning to their neighbours. And some had done more than warn. Indo-China was a suppurating sore. The Congofederation looked over desolation at the white dominance of South Africa. Tibet would never be the same again.

I warned them, he thought. I told them years ago what must happen but what did they do? Ignored me, of course, what else? I was just one man crying in the wilderness — an irritating voice, good for a few laughs and not much else. But Geldray listened, he told himself. And

21

Michele. And Easton. They listened and they believed.

He looked up to where the ship towered against the sky.

The means by which they hoped to save the human race.

2

The woman was young, attractive, completely naked. She had been cleaned inside and out and was ready to be frozen but, despite scopolamine, she was still tense and afraid.

'I'm not so sure, Doctor,' she said and sat upright on the wheeled stretcher. 'I don't think I want to go through with it.'

'Why not?'

'Well, there's a risk, isn't there? I mean, there's no guarantee that I'll live through it. Anyway,' she added firmly. 'I've changed my mind. I don't want to go now. I'd rather stay here.'

'Are you sure?'

'Yes, Doctor. I'm quite sure.'

It's some man, thought Celia. Someone she thinks she's in love with. Or maybe we caught her on the rebound from some broken affair. Whatever the reason she doesn't want to go. Not that I blame her, she thought. With her face and figure life could be a ball. And what have we really got to offer her? A chance to start from scratch on some new world. A fifteen per cent chance that she'll die in transit. No wonder she doesn't want to go.

'You do understand, Doctor?' The woman was anxious.

'Of course I understand,' said Celia, and smiled to show that she meant it. 'Now why don't you just relax,' she suggested. 'There's nothing to be afraid of.'

'You don't mind? About my quitting, I mean?'

'Why should I?' The hypogun made a soft hiss as it blasted pentathol into the woman's bloodstream. Five seconds later she was blissfully unconscious. She would stay that way until resurrected. Or until she was dead.

I'm getting as bad as the others, thought Celia. Morals, ethics, consideration for the feelings of others, all have gone to the wall. Only one thing matters now — to get the ship loaded and on its way.

She looked up from the woman as a

heavy door swung open and Jud Barman, bulky in his protective clothing, entered the compartment.

'Is this the last?' The biomech looked tired. He had been working for a long period in sub-arctic conditions and the strain was beginning to tell. 'Well?' he snapped impatiently. 'Answer me. Is it?'

She bridled and then made a conscious effort to relax. A biological mechanic was to a doctor as a doctor was to a nurse — and she had snapped at plenty of nurses in her time.

'The last of the present batch,' she said, and stood, shivering in the stream of frigid air welling into the room. Beyond the open door stood the tiered compartments where frozen humans rested in their amniotic tanks. Those tanks were filled with liquid helium. Ice was red hot by comparison. 'How many as yet?'

'A hundred and ninety-three.'

'Is that all?' She remembered the woman and her belated fears. 'Are many quitting?'

'Too many,' said Barman grimly. 'We'll have to do something about it if it keeps up.' He dropped gloved hands to the stretcher, aimed it at the open, insulated door. 'How about promoting some coffee while I put this baby to bed?'

She returned with the coffee as he was climbing out of his furs. He sniffed at the black liquid. 'Brandy?'

'A little. For medical reasons. You need it. You know,' she said, sitting, 'you hyper-professionals make me smile. Don't you know anything of the dangers of working for too long in low temperatures? Frostbite, for example?'

'That's your department,' he said. 'Give me a brain to repair, a nervous system to check, a gland to investigate with radioactives and I'm your man. Cuts and bruises I leave to you.' He sipped appreciatively at the coffee. 'This is good. Where did you find the brandy?'

'Trebor had a bottle tucked away in the farm.' She looked thoughtfully at the door behind which lay the honeycomb. 'Tell me, Jud. Do you honestly believe the world is going to a radioactive hell?'

'Geldray does.'

'I know. So does Dolman. Do you?'

26

'If you mean that the world as we know it is going to change,' he said slowly, 'then yes, I do. If you mean that the human race is due to become extinct, well, I'm not so sure. It might not be human as we know it,' he added. 'Mutation can produce some queer things, but they'll be the direct descendants of our own stock.

'Look at it this way,' he said. 'In the Middle Ages the Black Death wiped out a third of the population of Europe. No matter how you look at it that's a hell of a death-rate. But, in the long run, it simply didn't matter. Not to civilization or the race. The Indian tribe living in Terra del Fuego were almost wiped out by kindness. Someone gave them some blankets to keep them warm. They didn't know the blankets were infected with smallpox. Those Indians almost became extinct. They had no natural defence against the disease and so almost all of them died. Almost. That's the point. It seems that no matter what the disease or catastrophe some manage to survive. Always.'

'That's a comforting philosophy,' she

said. 'But it simply isn't true.'

'So?'

'So none of them survived. And, even if what you say is true, there always has to be a first time.'

'That's right,' he admitted.

'And this,' she pointed out, 'could be it.'

'Yes,' he said. 'It could be. That's why I'm going with the ship.'

* * *

The man was small, stooped, looking every day of his sixty-three years but his eyes were still bright and his voice firm. 'Now,' said Professor Jacques Michele. 'I want you to observe.'

George Longridge obediently hunched a little closer to the older man. They stood beside one of the splayed legs of the vessel, the gaping orifices of the venturies far above their heads. A strut had been temporarily attached to the leg with suckers. From the strut hung a chain supporting a ten-pound weight. The weight rested in the bowl of an ordinary kitchen scale. The chain hung slack over the edge of the bowl.

'Now,' said Michele. His English was almost wholly free of Gallic inflexions. 'This is the final test. I make it as much to satisfy myself as you but it really is unnecessary. My theories have been proven correct too often for me to entertain any doubt as to the success of my drive.'

A hell of a time to entertain doubt, thought Longridge sourly. The ship built, almost completely loaded, and now he has to talk about doubting the drive. It's his way, he told himself. An eccentricity of age. The damn thing has been tested each way from Sunday.

He scowled to where an orange-painted truck stood patiently waiting at the far side of the ship. It carried radioactive slugs from the breeder pile situated far beyond the edge of town. I should be over there supervising the loading, he thought. Not standing here playing audience to a crazy old man. But, he told himself, the guy's not so crazy. His drive works and he can prove it. But why the hell did he insist on keeping on proving it?

'Now attend!' Michele spoke into a small radio. 'First stage!'

Nothing seemed to happen but the pointer of the scale moved across the dial so that, instead of registering ten pounds, it registered ten ounces.

'The ship now only weighs one-twentieth of what it did before,' said Michele cheerfully. 'The weight of the chain accounts for the discrepancy. As it only weighs twenty times as much the reactors will have twenty times the thrust. A simple matter of applied science, my friend.'

'Sure,' said Longridge.

'You are not impressed?'

'I'm busy. Those slugs have to be loaded and loaded right. I should be on the job. Hell,' he said, 'no one doubts that you've done a good job. Without your drive the ship would still be a dream on paper.'

'Yes,' said Michele.

'I'm glad we agree. Can I go now — teacher?'

'To play with radioactives?' Michele

shook his head. 'No, my young friend. Not you. Those others — what does it matter if they are rendered sterile by what they do? They are not going with the ship. But you — you are the man who will provide the power to send her to the stars.'

'Maybe.'

'You doubt?'

'Look,' said Longridge patiently. 'You've managed to develop an anti-gravity device. That alone would earn you a gaggle of Nobel prizes and about all the money there is in the National Bank. The rest?' He shrugged. 'Who knows?'

'I know!' snapped Michele. 'Listen! On Earth, because of the magnetic and gravitational field, we can reduce weight only as you have seen. In space we can reduce it still more. To nothing and less than nothing. I have proved this.'

'On paper?'

'In fact. With test models in space.'

'Models which vanished when the drive was turned full on,' said Longridge. 'Is that what we're going to do? Vanish?'

'From this universe, yes. How else can

it be? But there is nothing to fear. The ship will simply move to a place where negative weight is possible. Turn off the drive and it will return. But, in the meantime, it will have travelled faster than light itself.'

'All right,' said Longridge. 'I believe you.'

'But you are sure? You have no doubts?'

I've got a hell of a lot of doubt, thought Longridge. Sometimes I think I must be crazy to be willing to ride that crate, but where would I ever get another chance? And it's something new, he told himself. A chance to break out of the rut and go places, see things. Maybe I should have my head examined but it's too late to back out now. Not that I want to back out, he thought. I'm in it to stay.

'No,' he said. 'I've got no doubts.'

★ ★ ★

Each morning, shortly after dawn, David Easton had left his quarters and had been driven to the ship. Mostly he worked without pause until evening. Often he

32

greeted one dawn at his quarters and the following dawn at the ship. Time, to him, had become a succession of working periods broken at irregular intervals by the necessity to eat and sleep. He had lived this way the past three years of his life. Now it was over. For the past five days he hadn't left the ship at all. He doubted if he would again — on Earth.

From the upper entry-port of his command he stared at the township below. A jumble of hutments, workshops, unloading areas, and warehouses. All the things which went to make and supply a small industrial complex. A blunted spire rose above a roof of corrugated iron. A fenced area provided a playground for the tiny school. A cluster of women stood outside the commissary, their clothing eye-bright in the sun. Across the desert a single road cut a winding swathe. To one side the landing field looked like the scab of some exotic disease.

The place was alive with furious activity looking, at this height, like a disturbed ant hill, a rolling welter of apparently aimless but actually coldly functional movement. It was something which couldn't last.

We're killing it, he thought dispassionately. We're sucking it dry, draining it of life and vitality. When we're ready to leave it will be dying. After we've gone it will be dead. He had no regrets. The place existed to serve a purpose. Without the ship it would have no reason for being.

He stepped back and closed the port. A big man, hard, with the eyes and mouth of a cynic. Thirty-five years had given him little cause to be anything else. In that time he had met few men with ideals and dedication. Those few had built the ship. They had given him its command. He would kill anyone who tried to take it from him.

Adrienne Castle would help him do it. She was young, severe, red-headed, and intensely practical with an inner core of romanticism she did her best to hide. She looked up as he entered the computer-room buried deep in the heart of the ship. The computer was more than the heart — it was the brain.

'How's it going?' asked the captain.

'Not too bad.' She made adjustments, slender fingers moving with an electronician's skill. 'Want to try it?'

He nodded, spoke into a grille. 'Captain to pilot. Is the ship ready to leave?'

'No.' The voice was flat, cold, mechanical.

'Why not?'

'The hull is unsealed.'

'Where?' Easton looked baffled. 'In what manner is the hull unsealed?' he asked carefully.

'The lower, starboard entry-port.'

'Anywhere else?'

'The middle, port loading entry.'

'Damn!' Easton slammed his hand on the console. Of his own knowledge he knew of two more openings. 'This isn't good enough,' he said flatly. 'It's talking to a half-wit. Can't you do better than this?'

'I can. I have.' She smiled at his expression. 'It's only a computer,' she explained. 'Basically a simple mass of data. It can receive impulses, information, store it and use it a million times faster than any human but it hasn't got a brain. I just wanted to show you how I've improved it.'

'We've no time for games, girl,' he said harshly. 'I accept the fact that you know your job. I'll even give you praise if that's what you're after. But in return give me results. Results, damn it! Results!'

She flushed and stiffened. 'We have to start with the basics,' she said coldly. 'As a computer is designed to give information it is a relatively simple matter to make it give that information in a verbal form. After all, basic English consists of only eight hundred words; a normal vocabulary of about five thousand. To a machine that can handle millions of units of data that is nothing. The real problem lies in programming the instrument to volunteer information; to grasp the sense of a question and to anticipate further questions stemming from the original in the light of additional, required information. You follow?'

He nodded.

'As you said, in its basic state it has no more sense than a moron. Anticipatory sense, that is. It will answer any question truthfully but that is all.' She made further adjustments. 'I've cross-coupled banks of selected verbal-data together with suggestive circuits so that each question is investigated for total meaning. The machine has to cross-check a fantastic number of probabilities but that doesn't matter as it can do it so fast. The result is that each question is answered in anticipatory fullness instead of literal brevity. If you will try again?'

She's mad, he thought. She could skin me alive and roast me over a slow fire, but what the hell? I've no time for games or delicacy and she should know it. She should have more sense than to pick this time to show me how clever she is. 'Is the ship ready to leave?' he asked the pilot.

'No,' came the instant response. 'The hull is not yet airtight. It still has to be sealed at the lower, starboard entry-port, the middle, port loading entry, the — '

'That's enough,' he interrupted. 'You've done a good job,' he said to the girl. 'A damn good job.'

She didn't answer, too angry to be easily mollified.

'I mean it,' he insisted.

'Yes,' she said shortly. 'I suppose that you do. You'd be pleased with anyone who helped improve your ship.'

'All right,' he snapped, reflecting her anger. 'Sulk if you want to. But keep working. I want this thing to be fully operational by the time we're ready to leave. After all,' he reminded. 'Our lives are going to depend on it.'

'Yes, sir.' She was still cold.

'Oh, go to hell!' he said. And stormed from the compartment.

* * *

Trebor swore as he found the bottle, swore again as he inspected the contents. He hadn't taken a drink in three days and now this! Someone had moved it. Someone had taken a drink. A big one. That someone should be flayed and staked out on an ant hill.

He took a drink and felt the brandy burn its way to his stomach. The warmth relaxed him as he leaned back against the wall of the farm. Sombrely he looked at the vats and tanks, the chlorophyceae and yeasts, the mutated vegetation, the blowers and U.V. lamps of the farm. Food and fresh air for the entire ship and one of those it was meant for had sneaked in and snatched a drink from his private bottle. Not that he would ever go short. The waste-product of the yeast would see to that. But it wouldn't be the same. The brandy was ten years old.

He looked at the bottle and took another drink. Fred Trebor wasn't a drinking man, not to excess, but he liked to celebrate special occasions. In the past there had been too many of them but this was something different. The farm was now fully operational. The loading was almost finished. A solid week of non-stop effort had slowed a trifle and a man had the right to relax. Some men, that is. Not all. Not, for example, Lance Holmson. Never him.

The astronomer, thought Trebor, is a louse. A louse firstclass. A preaching S.O.B. who should have been drowned at birth. A blue-nosed creep if there ever was one. So the captain had put him in charge of weight-reduction seeing as how he had nothing special to do until they had some stars to check. But did he have to go snooping around like a dog in heat?

There was nothing wrong with those records, he told himself. A collection of jazz from way back, Armstrong, Waller, Gillespie, and Fitzgerald, a dozen more of the old masters, a connoisseur's delight. He had collected maybe a couple of hundred of them over the years. Holmson had dumped them. He had pointed out that the stuff was all on tape and could be played at any time. But tape wasn't the same. The records held memories, each scratch and chip was something individual. But trust a louse like Holmson to understand.

Trebor took another drink.

And the magazines, he thought. The special ones he'd saved since way back when. They couldn't be taped, damn it. They had gone for ever. To hell with Mr. Lance Holmson, he told himself. Just wait until he came round begging for a drink.

Just wait until that happy day.

The intercom buzzed. Trebor set down the bottle and jammed his thumb against the button. 'Farm. Trebor speaking.'

'Holmson here.' The astronomer's voice betrayed his fatigue. 'I've been checking the weight and find we've a little to spare. Is there anything special you need?'

'Sure.' Trebor was abrupt. 'I can use anything growable. Or,' he added, 'anything which can help to make things grow. Horse manure if you've got it.'

'I haven't got any of that.'

'You should have,' said Trebor bitterly. 'You're full of it.'

Holmson ignored the insult. 'I thought I'd ask,' he said. 'I'll load up with something useful, sugar, say. And Fred,' he hesitated. 'Those magazines I took from you. They were really quite heavy, you know. But I've had them all microfilmed. I'll see that you get the film and there are plenty of viewers you can use.' He waited. 'Fred?'

'I'm here,' said Trebor. He was breathing hard. Damn it! How easy it was to misjudge a man! 'That was decent of you,' he said. 'Real decent. I'll remember it.'

'There's no need,' said Holmson.

'Maybe not,' said Trebor. 'But if you ever want a drink you know where to come. Old farmer-boy will take care of you.'

'Thank you,' said Holmson. 'But I don't drink.'

'No,' said Trebor, and released the button. That's the trouble with you, he thought. There's too many things you don't do. A drink and a good woman would make a proper man out of you.

He lifted the bottle again and felt the warmth rise from his stomach to his brain. Women, he thought. That was the trouble with them — always a shortage.

He lowered the bottle as the door swung open without warning, almost choking in his haste to hide the evidence. They were still on the ground but living under ship-discipline and Easton could be a hell of a martinet. He relaxed as he recognized the intruder. 'Why the hell didn't you whistle?'

'Something wrong?' Doris Turner was the wrong side of forty but did her best to hide it. Usually she was successful but this wasn't one of those times. The chemist looked as she felt, dog tired. She looked interestedly at the farm and took a deep breath of the clean air. It was good air and carried the scent of growing things. 'Do you mind if I come in here?'

'Not while I'm around,' said Trebor. 'And as long as I'm not working on the cultures. I don't want to risk contamination,' he explained. 'So if you see a red light showing outside that is where you stay.' He remembered his manners. 'Want a drink?'

'I could use one,' she admitted. 'This has been one hell of a week.' She watched him find beakers and pour out what remained of the brandy. 'Thanks.'

They drank, she sipping, he gulping. A lush, she thought, and immediately corrected herself. Not a lush, she told herself. If he was he wouldn't be here. Just a man who has to drink because he's lonely. Because, when he drinks, he doesn't feel quite so lost, so much apart.

The stuff stops him remembering that he's really a failure.

Like I am, she thought. Someone with no family and no hope of ever getting one. No real friends, no home, nothing but an endless succession of rooming houses, cheap hotels, furnished apartments. No roots anywhere. No company but the people you work with. Nothing to do but work. So you become good at your work. Damn good. It's all you have.

She sipped at the brandy, feeling suddenly old and tired and close to tears.

That's why I'm here, she thought. That's why I'm going on this crazy adventure. Because the ship can be home and work and friends and a kind of family all rolled into one. Because here I'll be needed. Because here, maybe, I'll be really wanted. By him, perhaps?

She looked at Trebor over the edge of her beaker. We're of an age, she thought. I could be good for him, take him out of himself, help him relax so that he wouldn't have to lean so hard on the bottle. He shouldn't have to do that. No man should. 'Where are we going?' she asked. 'When we leave, I mean. Where are we heading?'

'I don't know,' he admitted. 'I haven't thought about it. Proxima Centauri, maybe, or Alpha Centauri. They are the nearest stars. But if they don't have habitable planets we'll have to keep on looking. Rigel, perhaps, or Sirius. Polaris or Vega. There's a lot of stars. The universe is a big place.'

'Damn big,' she agreed.

'It could take years,' he said. 'That's why the ship is self-contained. We can keep going until we all die of old age.'

'A nice prospect.' She sipped more of her brandy. 'But what if we don't find a planet suitable to set up the colony? What then?'

'We keep looking.'

'And if we still don't find anything?'

'We've got to,' he said. 'That's what this thing's all about.'

3

The church was dim and seemed cool because of that. It was an illusion; nothing made of corrugated iron in the full glare of the desert sun could be cool, but it was quiet and free from the general atmosphere of haste and tension outside. Lance Holmson liked the church. It was a place in which to sit and think and gain some kind of strength. A refuge against the cynicism and harshness of the outside world.

It's almost like an observatory, he thought. A place which dealt with things cool and calm and remote. A definite system of cause and effect which held all the answers if you only knew the right questions. Like mathematics, he told himself. Like the stars. Distant points which obeyed immutable laws. Indifferent to the emotional heat of men, the inconsistency of their behaviour. You knew where you were in an observatory, he thought. And you know where you are in a church.

A man stepped into the building, saw Holmson, stepped outside again. He was a tall man, stringy, with greying temples and a sun-scorched face. He was waiting, with others, when the astronomer left the building and stood, blinking in the sunlight, narrowing his eyes against the contrasting brilliance. 'Mr. Holmson.' He stepped a little forward. 'We've been waiting for you.'

'You have?' Holmson, his eyes now adjusted to the sunlight, recognized the man. He was a guard attached to the field. 'I know you. Ruben, isn't it?'

'That's right.'

'What do you want?'

'The answers to a few questions. The boys are getting a little anxious,' he explained. 'There are certain things they want to know. I thought it best to speak for them — you know how it is.'

'No,' said Holmson impatiently. 'I don't. Now if you will excuse me — ' He stepped forward, the guard didn't move. 'All right,' said Holmson resignedly.

'What is it you want to know?'

One of the other men shoved himself forward. 'Is it true that the ship's all ready to go?'

'Yes,' said Holmson. 'Theoretically, at least, we could leave at any time.'

'What happens to us when it does?'

'Nothing.' Holmson was impatient with ignorance. 'You may lose your jobs,' he said. 'But you knew that when you started.' He thought he knew what the man was driving at. 'You'll be safe,' he promised. 'You don't think we'd blast before you're all out of harm's way, do you?'

'To hell with all that,' snapped another man. 'I'm not worried about the ship. What about my daughter?'

'Your daughter?'

'Don't act so damned innocent!' snarled the man. 'You know what I'm getting at. She's on your ship, that's what. Kidnapped, by God! Well, we'll see about that.'

'Now take it easy, Zeth,' said the guard. 'We don't know about that.'

'His girl isn't the only one,' yelled a

man at the edge of the crowd. 'My son's vanished too.'

'Maybe they went off together?' suggested someone. The man spat his disgust.

'Went off where? Do you think I haven't looked? We've all been looking and what have we found? Nothing. There's only one place they can be — on that damned ship!'

Holmson appealed to the guard. 'Is it true what they're saying? About their children being missing, I mean?'

'It's true enough,' said the guard heavily. 'There are quite a few people missing these last few days. Young, mostly. Fit, healthy and active. Not kids. They've simply vanished.'

'And you think we have them on the ship?' Holmson's puzzlement was obviously genuine. 'That's ridiculous! We don't need them,' he explained. 'We couldn't take them if we wanted to. There simply isn't the room.'

'Maybe not,' admitted the guard. 'That's what I've been telling the boys but they don't want to listen. They're on the edge of getting nasty about it.' He lifted a hand and rubbed the back of his grizzled neck. Sweat made a dark patch under his arm. 'As I see it there's only one thing to do,' he said. 'We'll have to search the ship.'

'Impossible! The captain will never permit it.'

'No,' agreed the guard. 'I don't suppose he will. But he might change his mind if we tell him that we won't let you go until he does.'

He means it, thought Holmson. They all do. For the first time he felt afraid. They will keep me with them until they get their way, he told himself. And Easton will never let them get that. He can't have a gang of men stamping all over the ship. Not now. Not when we're sealed and all ready to go. I shouldn't have come out, he thought sickly. The orders were to stay inside. I've broken that order. Disobeyed. Easton will leave me behind without a second thought.

'Listen,' he said urgently. 'I appreciate your fears but, believe me, they're groundless. No one will get hurt when the ship leaves. No one is holding those missing people prisoner on the ship. Why,' he said, and managed to smile. 'The concept is ludicrous. Do you honestly think that I'd do a thing like that?'

The guard pursed his lips. 'Not you, maybe,' he admitted. 'But I wouldn't put it past the captain. Look at it our way,' he suggested. 'What else can we do?'

The sky cracked before Holmson could answer. The sonic bangs of aircraft dropping through the sound barrier echoed across the desert. A dozen shapes wheeled, circling over the town. The guard looked up, squinting, shielding his eyes with the flat of his hand. He swore wonderingly as the mushroom shapes of parachutes blossomed against the sky. 'What the hell goes on?'

'It's the army,' yelled a man then. 'No, it's not. It's the Citizens Corps. You can see the markings on the planes.'

'That's right,' said someone else. 'But what are they acting like this for?' He remembered the astronomer and swore when he discovered that he had gone. 'He'll reach the ship,' he said. 'He'll get

51

there before we can stop him.'

'Never mind,' said the guard. 'They won't be going anywhere now.'

* * *

Edward Smith had set up his command post at the edge of the landing field. Tensely he listened to the stream of reports coming from his squad-commanders; rapped a stream of orders to his reserves. 'Make sure those men covering the ship have rocket launchers aimed at the vessel. Take over the communications centre. Seal the road out of town. Put men around Geldray's administration block. Move, damn you! This isn't a game!'

Men saluted and raced away. Like tigers, he thought. Eager to show their strength. Eager, perhaps, to spill a little blood. Well, he thought grimly, that might happen soon enough. If Geldray and his men should be stupid enough to oppose him it would be reason enough. Violence, then, would be justified. The outraged will of the people showing those who had battened for so long on its financial blood that they were not sheep to be meekly sheared. They were tigers it was not safe to arouse. No, he thought. Not tigers. Keep it domestic. Catamounts would be better.

'Make sure the newsboys get full coverage,' he said to Tigue. 'Nothing detrimental, of course. Have some of the boys dish out candy bars and gum to the kids. Get some shots of the locals shaking hands with our people. We're liberators, remember that.'

'Sure,' said Tigue. He looked unhappy and a little foolish in his too-new uniform.

'Pick a couple of good-lookers, find some willing girls and pile on the cheesecake,' said Smith. 'And find someone with a grievance and have them tell it to the public. Pick a good one,' he added. 'Something juicy. Something with sex in it. Sex or violence. That always goes down well.'

'We've got to be careful about this,' said Tigue. He mopped his face, pale in the glare of the desert. 'You could be moving too fast.'

'We can't stand still,' reminded Smith.

'We've got to make an impact and this is it. A multi-billion dollar project,' he said. 'We've taken it over. It's in our hands. All we have to do now is to prove that we were needed. Not just on the corruption angle, that's a civilian matter, but as actual defenders of right and decency. If what we've heard is true that shouldn't be hard.'

'If it's true,' said Tigue. He sounded doubtful. 'Can we trust those men planted here?'

'Sure we can.' Smith was confident. 'I tell you, Harry, this is going to lift us right into the White House. Just make it sound good. That's your job,' he added. 'Do a good one.'

'I'll do my best.'

'Sure you will,' said Smith. 'If you don't you'll be dead.' He smiled so as to make it sound like a joke but it wasn't that. 'Keep in touch,' he ordered. 'I'm going to tackle Geldray.'

He found him waiting in the big office, sitting at his desk which was at an angle to the picture-window so that he could look at the ship by turning his head. He was alone. Smith spoke to his personal bodyguard. 'All right,' he said. 'You can wait outside.'

'Are you sure, Chief?' The bodyguard was young, eager, over-conscientious. 'He could have a gun in that desk. I'd better check.'

'Outside,' snapped Smith. 'Now!' He turned to find that Geldray was smiling at him. Well, he thought, let the old coot smile. He'll soon be smiling on the other side of his face.

'He could have been right,' said Geldray. 'What makes you so sure that he wasn't?'

'You won't kill me,' said Smith. He picked up a chair and carried it to the end of the desk so that he could see both desk and window. 'Your type doesn't go in for murder. And,' he added, 'even if you do have a gun in that desk you'll never get a chance to use it. You're old. You'd have to get it out, aim, and fire. All that will take time. I won't give you the time.' He sat down and lit a cigar.

Geldray looked down at his hands. They rested in full view on the top of his desk. 'I could have a foot-controlled weapon hidden in the woodwork,' he said mildly. 'But you've thought of that. That's why you chose a place to sit. And, I suppose, you're wearing full battle-armour under that fancy uniform.'

'Naturally.' Smith blew a streamer of smoke towards the window. 'I'm not a fool.'

'No,' said Geldray. 'I've never thought of you as that. As a mad, rabid dog, perhaps, but never as a fool.' He nodded to where armed members of the Citizens Corps ringed the ship. 'You must feel pretty strong to have tipped your hand like this. How do you think the government is going to react to this invasion by a private army?'

'They'll swallow it,' said Smith. 'They'll have to swallow a lot of things.'

'Any government is composed of men,' said Geldray. 'And men can be bought, blackmailed, or broken. They can even be killed. What are they going to call you?' he asked. 'Duce? Leader? Fuehrer? Chief? Chief,' he decided. 'It's domestic and it fits. 'Yes, Chief.' 'No, Chief!' 'Our beloved

Chief.' 'The Chief.'' He nodded. 'The first dictator of the United States of America.'

'Of the Federated Americas,' corrected Smith. 'Canada is so close already that a change of name will do it. Mexico won't stop us a day. The banana republics?' He shrugged. 'Just how long do you think they could stand against us?'

'And so Edward Smith, first Chief of the Federated Americas, will rule from Terra del Fuego to the North Pole.' Geldray didn't smile; there was nothing funny about it. 'Greenland?'

'Why beg for trouble?' asked Smith blandly. 'I'll be satisfied with the Americas — and you're going to help me get them. You and that ship out there.'

'No,' said Geldray.

'What you want has nothing to do with it,' said Smith cheerfully. 'I — ' He broke off as Tigue's voice whispered to him from the miniature radio-receiver planted behind his ear. He smiled as the voice finished what it had to say. 'By God!' he said. 'I couldn't have asked for anything better. Geldray, you've handed me the crown on a plate. Those missing people,' he explained. 'One of my agents sent word that feeling was running high against the ship. I figured that I'd have to fake some evidence but that isn't necessary now. Those people are on board the ship. They've been kidnapped and held prisoner.'

'Yes,' said Geldray.

'You admit it?'

'Why not? There's nothing you or anyone can do about it now.'

'You think not?' Smith's brain was burning as if on fire. The old fool had condemned himself out of his own mouth. This is it, he thought. This is what I've wanted. Doesn't the old fool guess that I'm recording all this? True, he reminded himself, what I said is on the tape too, but tapes can be edited so that doesn't matter. But that admission! Hell, this is my lucky day!

He pulled a folded paper from his pocket and held it between his fingers. 'This will stop you,' he said. 'An injunction signed by the Supreme Court. It grounds the ship. And,' he added, 'it authorises me to use any measures I see fit to make sure the order is obeyed.'

He threw it casually on the desk.

★ ★ ★

Geldray looked at it; a heavy, legal-looking document, the decoration of seals awesome in their significance. A ukase, he thought. A modern incantation. A combination of symbols signed by the highest in the land and supposedly effective because of that. But it's only a piece of paper, he told himself. Effective only if I'm willing to obey. Or can be forced to obey. 'Those people,' he said. 'Can you guess why I had them kidnapped and frozen in the honeycomb?'

'I don't give a damn,' said Smith.

'I want to give the colony the best chance I can.' Geldray turned his head, looked at the ship. 'We had a lot of unused space. Too many volunteers backed down at the last moment. I had to replace them somehow.'

'They'll make good witnesses,' said Smith. The tiny voice whispered in his

59

ear. 'We've got Dolman,' he told Geldray. 'Where's Michele?'

Geldray didn't answer.

'I suppose he's in the ship,' said Smith. 'It doesn't matter. We'll get him when we take it over.' He looked through the window to where it stood. 'You'd better tell them to open up and come out,' he said. 'Officers first, hands over their heads, no funny stuff or my boys will open fire. Tell them that.'

'Go to hell,' said Geldray.

'You don't like it?' Smith shrugged. 'I didn't think you would. But I didn't think you were stupid either. Personally I don't give a damn which way it goes. They can walk out or we can blast that thing and carry them out.'

'Or we can make a deal,' said Geldray quickly. 'I'm going to give you that chance. You want me on trial? All right, I'll co-operate to the full — if you let the ship go. I mean it,' he added. 'I'll play along all the way, give you all the facts you need.'

'I've got all the facts I need.'

'Maybe, but wouldn't you like me to

60

get up there and make a full confession? Dolman too. We'll do it,' he promised. 'We'll do anything you say — if you let the ship go.'

'Crawling, Geldray?'

'Call it what you like. Well?'

Smith shook his head. 'No,' he said. 'I don't have to make any deals. And I want those witnesses,' he explained. 'The ones on the ship.'

'I thought you'd say that,' said Geldray. He felt himself beginning to sweat. The cramp in his left leg was getting more than he could easily bear and the ache in his right knee, where it was crossed over the left leg and rammed up hard against the button beneath his desk, was, if anything, worse. 'I wish you hadn't,' he said. 'I had to try. Not for you or me but for all those people out there.' He nodded towards the window. 'I didn't want to have to kill them.'

'Kill them?' Smith straightened in his chair. 'What are you talking about?'

'The ship's got to have its chance,' said Geldray. He pressed his palms hard against the top of his desk. 'The human race has got to be given the chance to continue. You're not going to stop it. You can't stop it. Nothing can.'

'You're crazy!'

'This desk is booby-trapped,' said Geldray. 'There's a button underneath it. When you came into this room I pressed it. Since then I've kept it pressed by the pressure of my knee. It is hooked to a remote control apparatus. If released it will trigger off the ship's reactors. The crew are all settled for flight, they won't be hurt at all.' He paused. 'They won't be hurt,' he repeated. 'I wish I could say the same for those in the town.'

'You're bluffing,' said Smith. He swallowed, his face taut. 'Damn it, you're bluffing!'

'You rushed us,' said Geldray evenly. 'But, even so, you arrived too late. Ten hours ago you would have had us helpless. Now you've walked right into a trap. You can't get away in time,' he pointed out. 'You can't stop me. All I have to do is to lower my right knee. You must know what will happen then.'

It will be unleashed hell, he thought

dispassionately. The reactors were still 'dirty' and would stay that way for the first few hours of flight. The reaction mass was water. It would pass through the reactors and be heated to sun-fury. The ship would rise on a column of invisible, super-heated steam ejected at incredible velocity. The heat would be enough. The spread of the blast would flatten everything in the immediate vicinity of the ship. The radiation would take care of the rest.

As it rose the ship would kill the town.

'No!' Smith clawed at his holster. His gun came into view. 'Don't move! Stay exactly as you are! I'll kill you if you move!'

'Don't be idiotic,' said Geldray. 'If you shoot me I'll fall and the button will be released. I offered you a deal,' he said. 'I didn't want to kill the innocent people of this town. You've given me no choice.'

'There's always a choice,' said Smith. He was sweating. 'You don't have to kill anyone.'

'Crawling, Smith?'

'You old fool! I don't want to die!'

No, thought Geldray, you don't. Neither does anyone else but sometimes that price has to be paid for getting rid of mad dogs like you. Sometimes it's the only way. If more men were willing to die, he told himself, then freedom could be more than just a word. Men tolerated dictators because they loved life too much — more than they hated the loss of their liberty. Not, he reminded himself, that they had ever had it. Not real liberty. Not true freedom.

Maybe those in the ship would be able to work something out, he thought. Something new, free of the dead-weight of old traditions and conservatism. At least they would be free to try. He could give them no more than that.

'You're bluffing,' said Smith firmly. 'You wouldn't kill the town and you wouldn't kill yourself. You must be taking me for a fool.'

'What have I to lose?' asked Geldray. 'But you're right in one thing — I don't want to kill innocent people.'

'No,' said Smith. 'I didn't think you would.' He reached for his collar, easing it as if he found the heat of the office oppressive. 'Harry,' he said sharply into his radio. 'Harry? Damn you, answer me!'

'Don't do it,' said Geldray.

Smith ignored him. 'Harry. Blast the ship. Get the boys to fill it full of holes. Yes, you fool! Now. Right away. Hurry!'

'No,' said Geldray.

And released the button.

4

The air held a peculiar thickness; the impression of greyish solidarity which should have been opaque but somehow wasn't. A transparent mist of innumerable particles in continuous agitation. It reminded Easton of a magnified Brownian movement of the very constituents of the atmosphere. He blinked but it stayed the same.

It's my eyes, he thought dully. They must have been damaged in some way. The capillaries of the retina ruptured perhaps. The take-off was too savage, he told himself. We must have hit twenty gravities before I blacked out. The instrumentation must be all to hell.

He lay for a long while thinking about it. Vaguely he was aware of his body. He felt pain, not the sharp agony he had experienced during the ascent, but the dull, nagging ache of bruised bones and muscles. He closed his eyes. The darkness made things seem worse and he opened them again. He decided to rise.

'God!' The voice belonged to Longridge. 'My eyes! What — ?'

'Take it easy,' said Easton. He unsnapped the restraints and swung his legs over the edge of the couch. He sat upright and felt a sudden nausea.

'What the hell goes on?' There was a threshing as Longridge moved on his couch. 'Jesus!'

'I told you to take it easy,' snapped Easton. He sat quietly, breathing deeply, waiting for the sickness to pass. His eyes hurt and there was a thin, high-pitched ringing in his ears that he hadn't noticed before. 'Don't move too fast,' he warned. 'Take time to get adjusted.'

'This is crazy,' said Longridge. Like the captain he sat on the edge of his couch. 'What's happened to everything? It looks all different.'

'Yes,' said Easton. He looked carefully around. The control room had changed. The shape was wrong; the height, the proportions, the instruments, everything. Straight lines were curved, flat surfaces bowed. It was like looking into a distorting mirror. He rose and stumbled towards the controls. 'Captain to pilot,' he said, slumping into the control chair. 'Report.'

'In detail?'

'In full detail. I want to know what's happened.'

'We left the field at maximum acceleration,' said the pilot. 'It was essential to avoid all threat of damage to the hull. At a height of twenty-six thousand miles we came into the range of an armed space station. It fired an atomic missile. I had no alternative but to follow my programming which is to safeguard the ship at all costs. Therefore — '

'Wait a minute,' interrupted Easton. 'Are you sure about that?'

'My programming? Quite sure.'

'I meant the atomic missile. Are you certain there was one?'

'Yes. I tracked its radio-guide carrier beam. It was directed on a course which would have intercepted our own.'

'Nice,' said Longridge from where he sat listening. 'That louse Smith must have had a friend commanding that station.'

Maybe, thought Easton. That or every station had been alerted to fire on the ship. He spoke again to the pilot. 'How did you manage to avoid the missile?'

'I immediately engaged the full extent of the drive. We are now in what I have been programmed to refer to as M-space.'

'And,' said Easton tightly, 'just where the hell is that?'

'I do not know,' said the pilot precisely. 'I am not familiar with the region but I can tell you how we came to enter it. Full engagement of the drive results in the ship acquiring negative mass with relation to the normal universe. Such a state cannot naturally exist. To avoid a paradox the ship was forced to move to a region where it can. This region I have been programmed to refer to as M-space.'

'So you told me,' said Easton.

'I have no means of describing the region other than by analogy,' said the pilot. 'Imagine a two-dimensional spiral. A journey from one point on the line of the spiral to any other point must be made by following the line. That is travel in normal space. M-space enables the ship to travel directly across the spiral. Do you understand?'

'I think so.'

'Imagine an insect,' said the pilot. 'It is on one side of a page in a book. It wants to get to the other side of the page. To do so it must travel completely to the edge, cross it, and then proceed down the other side. If it could penetrate the paper, bore right through it, that would be travel in M-space.'

'All right,' said Easton. 'That's enough. What about the distortion we are experiencing? The peculiarity of the air?'

'I have no organic means of checking what you say,' said the pilot. 'However it is possible that, because of different frames of reference, your sensory apparatus may need time in order to adjust to the new conditions. Would you like to see outside?'

'Yes,' said Easton. He stared at the soft, coiling greyness pictured in the screens. 'Well?'

'Can you see nothing?'

'Only a mass of grey swirl. Are the receptors in order?'

'Yes.' The pilot sounded thoughtful. 'It could be that your sensory apparatus is functioning but your brain cannot correlate the data with which it is supplied,' it suggested. 'Naturally, I have no means to check whether this is so.'

'Never mind,' said Easton. 'Don't worry about it.'

'It may be possible for me to filter the incoming data so as to present it in a more easily recognizable form,' said the pilot. 'I would have to work on the basis of acceptable-analogues and I shall need further extensions similar to those which enable me to relay information in a verbal manner.'

'Leave it for now,' said Easton. 'How is the ship?'

'In peak condition and wholly functional,' said the pilot. It paused. 'I have received an urgent message for you.'

'Well?' Foreboding sharpened Easton's voice. 'Spill it, damn you! What's the message?'

'You are needed in the hospital,' said

71

the machine coldly. 'Professor Michele is dead.'

* * *

He looked very small lying on the plastic top-sheet of the cot. Small and old and fragile. Too fragile, thought Easton as he looked down on the shapeless mound beneath the thin cover. His strength rested in his intellect. Now it's gone together with the thing which made him unique, an individual. Now he's nothing but broken bones and a mess of tissues and fluid. A dollar's worth of chemicals, he told himself. The basic worth of any man.

'How did it happen?' he asked, not looking up.

'We don't know for sure,' said Jud Barman. He stood washing his hands at a tap. He shut off the water, stepped on a pedal, let hot air dry his fingers. 'I was with Celia on the couches in the operating theatre. He was in here on one of the cots. They're just as good as the couches,' he explained. 'We designed them that way.'

'I know that,' said Easton impatiently. 'What happened?'

'He must have left his couch, gone for a drink or something,' said Barman. 'My guess is that he never made it back. He was on the floor when we found him.' He looked down at the body. 'Pelvis broken,' he said flatly. 'Spleen ruptured and multiple lesions of the intestines. His thorax is the real mess. Ribs snapped and driven into the heart and lungs. He wasn't strong to begin with. He couldn't hope to withstand the weight of twenty others piled one on top of the other. Not while lying on the floor.'

'I doubt if any of us could,' said Easton. 'Where's Celia?'

'Lying down. She was pretty sick when she woke and finding Michele didn't help. I gave her a sedative and sent her to rest.' Barman blinked his eyes several times in succession. 'It's getting better,' he said. 'The distortion, I mean. It's either going or I'm getting used to it.'

'You're probably getting used to it,' said Easton. He looked down at Michele. 'Can't you do anything for him?'

'No.' Barman was positive. 'He's been dead too long,' he explained. 'The brain has degenerated. If I could have got to him in time I could have hooked him into a life-support apparatus. By-passed his heart and lungs while I operated and maybe used prosthetic implants. I could even have amputated his body and kept his head alive with an artificial analogue. But not now,' he said regretfully. 'It's too late. Even freezing him would be a waste of time. He's gone too far.'

Gone and soon to be forgotten, thought Easton. But not by me. Not when I'm commanding a ship fitted with his drive. Not when I know next to damn all about that drive. Why? he asked himself in sudden anger. Why does a man so intelligent have to be such a fool? He knew that we could take-off at any moment. We all knew it. Why the hell did he suddenly decide to get a drink? Why the hell did he have to get himself killed?

'Do you want to keep him?' asked Barman. 'There's plenty of room in the honeycomb if you do. Too much damn room,' he said bitterly. 'Those few couples we managed to snatch didn't go far. If you want to keep him you can. Not,' he added, 'that it will do any good. He can't be resurrected.'

'Freeze him,' decided Easton. 'He's earned the right to be buried in dirt,' he explained. 'We'll keep him until we find some.'

★   ★   ★

Holmson entered the control room. He looked pale and a thin trace of blood still discoloured his nostrils. He winced as he sat in a chair. 'You wanted me?'

'That's right,' said Easton. He turned from the controls and looked critically at the astronomer. The man was in a bad way but there was no time to be gentle. 'How are you feeling now?'

'I'll manage.' Holmson lifted a hand to his temple, rubbed hard against the bone. 'What did you want to see me about?'

'I want to know where we are,' said Easton. 'The pilot can't tell us. It took off on remote control and the only instruction it had was to get us off the field and away from danger. To do that and do it fast.'

'It did that right enough,' said Longridge sourly. Gingerly he felt his ribs. 'Too damn fast.'

Easton ignored the interruption. 'The pilot did what it was told to do,' he said. 'But no one thought to give it a destination. Now we have to find out how far we've travelled, how fast we're travelling and where we are heading. I want the answers to those questions,' he told Holmson. 'Those and a few more. I want you to get them.'

Holmson lowered his hand. 'We'll have to find some recognizable objects,' he said thoughtfully. 'Some of the more prominent stars.' He looked at the screens. 'We can't do that here.'

'Not while we're in M-space,' agreed Easton. 'I know that. I was waiting until you were fit to take observations.' He turned to the controls and look a deep breath. 'All right,' he told the pilot. 'Sound the take-off warning. I want everyone strapped down tight.' He fastened his own restraints as the others hit

76

the couches. Ten seconds later the warning siren fell silent. 'Pick the most opportune moment consistent with safety,' he told the pilot. 'Then cut the hi-drive.'

He forced himself to relax in the chair, glad the others couldn't see his face. We could come out in the heart of a planet, he thought. Right in the guts of a star. We could appear directly in the path of a comet, a meteor, or other lump of galactic debris. Or maybe we won't come out at all. Damn Michele, he thought. He told us too much and yet not enough. He didn't tell anyone enough. Maybe he didn't know it to tell, he reminded himself. He was working on pure theory and he was scared of losing his secret. While he held it he was safe against leaks, assured of being allowed to come with the ship. Well, he had come and what good had it done him?

'Now,' said the pilot.

There was a twisting, a strange sensation of rotary movement, a horrible outside-in folding as if everything had been forced through an unguessable dimension. A sharp odour filled the air and the metal of the ship sang with released energy. There was a sudden, shocking vertigo and a stabbing discomfort of the eyes. Then it was over. Stars shone with their normal brilliance from the screens. The odd distortion of familiar shapes lingered a moment then vanished as their eyes adjusted to accustomed frames of reference.

'All right,' said Easton. 'Let's get to work.'

* * *

Trebor measured out the inverted sugar, the citric acid, the nutrient, and the flavouring. He topped up the five-gallon container with water, checked that the thermostat was holding at blood-heat and gently added the yeast. 'There you are, baby,' he murmured. 'Eat well and grow hearty.' Deftly he rammed home the fermentation lock and filled the twisted glass tube with sterilizing fluid.

'Do you honestly think there's a danger of vinegar fly in this place?' Doris had entered the farm and was watching Trebor at work.

'What's that?' He turned, startled, then relaxed as he saw who it was. 'Doris, how often must I tell you? Whistle before you come bursting in here.'

'You could have locked the door,' she pointed out. 'Or switched on that red light.' She stepped forward to peer at what he'd been doing. 'Something special?'

'That's going to be champagne,' he said. 'As near to the real stuff as you can get. I want it ready to celebrate our landing.'

'You're crazy,' she said. 'It takes months to make that stuff.'

'Years,' he admitted. 'But not with this yeast. It's a specially mutated strain with the appetite of a tiger. It'll convert that sugar before you know it. Then I'll centrifuge the wine to clarify it, age it by electrolysis, add carbon dioxide to give it a sparkle. I'll tell you what,' he added. 'If you can honestly tell the difference between this and the real thing I'll eat the bottle.'

'Fair enough,' she said. 'But why go to all that trouble? Why not just freeze out the alcohol and done with it?'

'Please,' he said. 'We're not talking about hooch. This is going to be one hundred per cent genuine champagne.' They both laughed. 'Is this an official visit?' he said. 'Or did you just drop in to keep me company?'

'I just felt like talking.' She sat on the edge of his work-bench and shivered. 'You know, this travelling is giving me the creeps. I keep wondering what's outside, waiting, maybe, to break in.'

'And everytime we cut the drive you wonder if we're going to stay in one piece.' He nodded. 'I know. I've thought about it too. I guess everyone has. But we've got the problem licked now. Holmson figured out where we are and checked with the pilot. Those test runs gave us our speed of travel. All we have to do now is to aim the ship, engage the hi-drive, wait and then come out again for another look round. Simple.'

'Sure,' she said. 'I know that. But there's something else bothering me.

What if we aren't alone out here? What if we bump into another race? What then?'

'I don't know,' he admitted. 'I guess that we either get friendly or tear each other apart. Or,' he added, 'we could just ignore each other.'

'We couldn't do much else,' she pointed out. 'The ship isn't armed for special warfare. If we ran into anything we'd be a sitting target.' She chewed thoughtfully at her thumbnail. 'Do you think we might?' she asked. 'Meet someone else out here, I mean. Is it possible?'

'Certainly it is.'

'I mean really possible,' she insisted. 'Not highly probable.'

'I know what you mean,' he said. 'If you want the exact odds I can give them to you.' He frowned, remembering. 'About one in four hundred light years,' he said. 'An intelligent race, I mean. They are scattered about four hundred light years apart.'

'You're joking.'

'No,' he said. 'I mean it. It's all been worked out. Professor Carl Sagan did it years ago. He worked on the premise that matter is continually being created and that ten new stars are being formed each year. From that he extrapolated there would be ten new planetary systems as each star would have planets. Each system would support one life-form and of those life-forms one in ten would be intelligent. Each ten years one of those intelligent life-forms would reach a technological civilization comparable to our own. He assumed that there could be well over a million such races existing at this present time. A million races scattered throughout the galaxy means that there is one about every four hundred light years.'

Doris frowned as she thought about it. 'Four hundred light years,' she murmured. 'That's a hell of a lot of space.'

'Yes,' said Trebor.

'And it's really all speculation,' she said. 'There's no real proof.'

'It depends on what you mean by proof,' said Trebor. 'If you want to you can read a lot in the ancient writings and legends. They could mean that, in days gone past, extraterrestrial races contacted our own. But if you mean actual, present-day proof, no, we haven't any. But Sagan did a good job on the maths and, accepting his premise, it makes sense.'

'A lot of things make sense,' she said. 'It makes sense that a man can't fly but things aren't always what they seem. Anyway,' she said, 'let's drop the subject. Aren't you going to offer me a drink?'

'You'd like one?' He stooped and rummaged under the workbench. When he rose he was flushed. 'Gin,' he said. 'It's all I have left.'

'Gin will do fine.' She watched as he sorted out a couple of beakers. Like a boy, she thought. Clumsy in his eagerness to please. Refusing to anticipate because of fear of rejection. Someone's hurt him in the past, she told herself. Hurt him so badly that he's scared of being hurt that way again. But he doesn't have to be scared of me. 'Haven't you forgotten something?' she said as he handed her a beaker.

'Forgotten?'

'That light outside the door,' she said. 'The one that tells everybody to stay outside.' Her eyes held his, her hand was soft against his own. 'We don't want to be interrupted, do we?'

'No,' he said thickly. 'We don't.'

* * *

The cabin was warm, close, dark. Like a womb, thought Easton. The only really safe place anyone knows in his entire life. To be protected and cared for without a worry in the world. Not, he told himself, until close to the end when you get thrown out into an inhospitable environment. No wonder babies cried. They had something to cry about.

He turned restlessly on his cot. He was overtired, his brain on fire with vagrant thoughts and images. He could have taken a sedative but who could tell when there might not be an emergency? What good would he be then if drugged and unconscious? He stretched, his head touching metal, hearing the soft, almost inaudible sound of the ship. The drive was strongest, a thin, high-pitched singing like a vibrating crystal. The air-conditioners made a deeper purr. Beneath them, a muted susurration of noise, came the general sounds of living humanity.

The ship is an egg, he thought. Filled with potential life and ready to explode into growth at the touch of a favourable environment. A spermatozoon, he told himself. Ejected from Earth and now seeking an ovum to fertilize. A new planet to bear the race of Man.

He turned again, then stiffened, lying with eyes wide, ears strained, tense in the darkness. It came again, a small, metallic sound. He sat upright as the door slid open and a shape entered the room. He reached out and gripped smooth, soft flesh. 'Adrienne!'

'I — ' She caught her breath. 'I didn't know that you were awake,' she said. 'I — '

'Is anything wrong?' His hands tightened with nervous anxiety. 'Quick, girl! Is anything wrong?'

'No,' she said, and then, 'Please! You're hurting me!'

'Sorry.' He released his grip. Swinging his legs over the edge of the cot he rose, shut the door, snapped on the light. He was naked aside from the pants of his pyjamas. 'You should have knocked,' he said. 'You should have waited for me to answer. You shouldn't have come creeping in here the way you did.'

'I know,' she admitted. 'It was foolish of me.' She stood before him, her bare forearms red where he had gripped, neat and slim in her white, laboratory smock. Her hair was very red, her skin very white. She wore a perfume which held the scent of carnations and her lips glistened as if with oil. 'I was passing,' she explained. 'I thought I heard you call out. I wondered if anything was wrong.'

'There's nothing wrong.' He stood, looking at her, conscious of her attraction. She's beautiful, he thought. Under that façade of hard, functional severity, she is really beautiful. He felt a sharp regret at the years he had wasted, the years he could have spent with someone like her — if he had found someone like her. 'How is the pilot? Did you finish running those checks I asked for?'

'Yes.' She turned and sat on the edge of the cot. 'There is nothing wrong with the computer. The mathematics of M-space are different to those of our own universe, that's all. Time seems to be a variable.' She looked up at him, at his face, his shoulders, his naked torso. 'You're worried,' she said flatly. 'I can tell. Well, so am I.'

'About the same thing?'

'The journey is taking too long,' she said. 'We've a means of travelling much faster than light and yet things aren't working out as they should. Each time we engage the hidrive we hit the unpredictable. The jumps aren't of even length even though, as far as we know, they are of the same duration.'

'So?'

'So I think the drive could be failing, breaking down. There could be something we know nothing about, a tolerance level we can't even guess at, some sort of malfunctioning we can't suspect. I've been wondering,' she said, 'about what would happen if, one day, we tried to engage the drive and nothing happened. What then?'

'We live, breed, exist and die in the ship,' he said curtly. 'It's a self-contained world. Our descendants may be able to reach an habitable planet.'

'There's an alternative,' she suggested. 'Two in fact. We could go back, try to reach Earth before it was too late. Or,' she said slowly, 'we could try to resurrect Michele's brain.'

'You've been talking to Barman,' said Easton. 'This is his idea.'

She nodded.

'He told me that it couldn't be done,' said Easton. 'He said that degeneration had made it impossible.'

'He still says so.' Adrienne looked down at her knees, smooth and white beneath the hem of her smock. 'The ego of Michele, the personality, is dead. But the information carried in his brain might still be available. Barman reckons that it's worth trying.'

He would, thought Easton. Any excuse so that he can play with flesh and blood as if he were playing with machines. But that was unfair. To Barman people were machines. Protoplasmic devices of remarkable efficiency, but still machines. And Michele, the real Michele, was dead. What harm could Barman do?'

'All right,' he said. 'I'll let him make the attempt. It'll keep him out of mischief.'

'You don't like him very much, do you?'

'He's efficient,' said Easton cautiously.

'That isn't answering the question.'

Damn you and your questions, he thought savagely. What has liking got to do with it? I took what I could get. A drunken farmer, a biomech who had stepped too often across the accepted boundary, an adventure-hungry engineer, an idealistic doctor, a love-starved chemist, a fanatic as an astronomer and you, what are you? A frustrated female sublimating her sexual needs in work?

'I'm tired,' he said. 'Too tired to play stupid games.'

'You want me to go?'

He saw the expression on her face, the shock of rejection. I've hurt her, he thought. Damn it, I'm always hurting her.

89

But if I let her get too close the hurt will be deeper, stronger, harder to bear.'

She rose, stepped towards the door, passing very close to where he stood. She reached the panel, opened it, stepped outside. She hesitated, one hand preventing the door from closing. 'David.'

'What is it?'

'I didn't hear you call out,' she said. 'You know that?'

'I know it.'

'Then — ?'

'Goodnight, Adrienne,' he said. And closed the door firmly between them.

5

The planet was a cloud-hidden ball, an astronomical unit and a quarter from a yellow, G-type sun. It had a moon, an atmosphere close enough to that of the Earth, a gravity a little higher. It promised to be a place where they could live.

Longridge looked at it as it hung in space a hundred thousand miles below the orbiting vessel. 'Home,' he said. 'It doesn't look like home, does it?'

'It's not Earth,' said Easton shortly. But, he thought, no other planet could ever be Earth, though it had seas and clouds, mountains and ice-caps, islands and continents. No other planet could have the shared beginnings of all living things. But this planet was going to be their home. 'Where's Holmson?' he said.

'Getting ready.' Longridge turned from where he stood before the screens. 'Why don't you let me go down?' he suggested. 'I've flown before. I can handle the auxiliary.'

'We can all handle it,' said Easton. 'But that isn't the point. Holmson is expendable,' he pointed out. 'If anything should happen we lose an astronomer but that's all.' He frowned as he studied the unbroken clouds wreathing the planet below. 'We've got to know what's under there,' he said. 'If there isn't any vegetation we're wasting our time. If it's too hot the same. Damn it,' he said. 'It could be like Venus. All cloud and red hot at ground level. A high-pressure dust-bowl. We've got to be sure.'

'We could drop a probe,' suggested Longridge. 'I could rig up something.'

'We could do a lot of things,' agreed Easton. 'But we're going to send down Holmson in an auxiliary.' He turned as the astronomer entered the control room. 'Ready?'

'As much as I'll ever be,' said the astronomer. He looked squat, bulky in his high-G suit. 'Do I go alone?'

'Can you manage it alone?'

'Yes. It only takes one man to handle an auxiliary.'

'Then you'll go alone,' said Easton flatly. 'I don't want to waste time rousing a crew from the honeycomb. Now listen,' he said. 'We've only got two auxiliaries so I want you to be careful. Your mission is to make a preliminary survey of what's down there. Go under the clouds and look around. If you see a suitable spot to land the ship I want to know it. Look for signs of habitation, cities, cultivated fields, things like that. Try and get an idea of the various zones. Look for distinguishing rivers. Go in fast, keep moving, don't let yourself get distracted.'

'Just a quick once-over to get the general picture?'

'That's about it. Don't land. Don't take any chances. Keep in continuous radio contact with the ship. Keep up a running commentary. Never mind if you think you have nothing to say that's important; just keep talking. Understand?'

Holmson nodded.

'All right,' said Easton. 'Get to it.'

'There goes a happy man,' said

Longridge enviously as Holmson left the room. 'At least he's getting his teeth in some action.'

'Your turn will come,' said Easton. 'Now get on that radio.'

He sat, waiting, striving to be patient. We've waited a long time, he thought. Too long. Then more waiting while we jumped closer to this system, a longer wait while we manoeuvred for orbit, more waiting while we checked on what we could see. Now it can't be much longer. Soon we'll know. One way or the other we'll know.

His hands began to tremble and he clenched them, locking the fingers together. Please, God, he thought, let this be it. Let this planet be one we can live on. Please, God, let it be that!

'He's going down,' said Longridge. He wore headphones and was taping the communication. 'You want to hear this?'

'Not yet.' Until he reached the clouds there could be nothing but routine gossip.

'Nothing much to hear,' said Longridge. He looked thoughtful. 'What if he finds something down there? A civilization of sorts. What then?'

Easton shrugged.

'We'd have to work something out,' mused Longridge. 'Maybe swap them technical knowhow in exchange for food and stuff. Hey,' he said. 'We could even become the king-pins of the whole set-up. You know, gods from the sky and all that.'

'Where's Holmson now?'

'On the edge of the atmosphere,' said Longridge. He listened. 'He wants to know should he collect samples?'

'Hell, yes!' snapped Easton. 'As many as he can get. Damn it, do I have to teach him his job now?' He waited until Longridge had relayed the instructions. 'Put it on,' he ordered. 'Let me hear what he has to say.'

' . . . atmosphere's beginning to thicken now,' said Holmson's voice from the speaker. 'Some temperature rise but nothing serious.' A pause. 'Sample taken. Am going to reduce forward speed.' The dull scream of braking jets echoed from the speaker.

'Can you spot him?' Adrienne had entered the control room. She leaned

95

forward, examining the screens. A tiny black fleck traced a path across the milky globe beneath.

' . . . dropping lower now, well down into the clouds,' said Holmson's voice. 'It's very thick and I can't see a thing. Altitude fifteen thousand.'

'Can you see anything?' Longridge leaned closer to the microphone. 'Any sign of civilization?'

'Nothing. I've just entered the dark side and it's as black as the inside of your head. I'm flying by instruments alone. The radar says there's nothing ahead of me, maybe I'm crossing an ocean. I certainly hope so. If there are any sizable mountains here I don't want to hit them.'

Easton looked down at his hands. The knuckles were white with strain. Deliberately he unlocked his fingers.

'I've reached the day side,' said Holmson. 'I'm well below the clouds which look like a ceiling of mother-of-pearl. The air is very thick. I've reduced speed so as to make out the terrain.'

'Yes?' Longridge was eager.

'No cities, roads or cultivated fields as far as I can see. I'm crossing a wide lake now. Beyond there are forests, great trees looking something like cyclads. Two rivers meet way back in some low hills. There is a great plume of smoke to the north. It could be the sign of an active volcano. The ground seems firm and level.'

'Any game trails?'

'None that I can see. There's a valley to the south,' continued Holmson. 'A range of low mountains to the north. There are outcroppings covered with vegetation. There's a river with a wide loop just ahead. There's something within that loop. It looks as if it could be a clearing.'

'I want to know more about that,' said Easton. 'Tell him to find out about it. Circle if he has to. Hurry!'

'Approaching the clearing now,' said Holmson. 'I can see buildings of some kind. 'I — ' He broke off, gasping.

'What is it?' said Longridge. 'Keep talking, damn you!'

'I don't believe it,' said Holmson. 'It's impossible! I just can't believe it! There's — '

The voice died. The swollen bulk of the planet vanished. The hatefully familiar distortion of M-space filled the ship.

★ ★ ★

'Damn!' Easton spun in his chair and snapped at the pilot. 'Cut the hi-drive! Immediately!' He fought the nausea of transition. 'Keep in touch with Holmson,' he said to Longridge. 'Maintain contact.'

'I'm trying!' The engineer scowled as he adjusted the radio. 'I can't get anything,' he complained. 'Not a damn thing.'

'Keep at it.' Easton turned and looked at Adrienne. 'There's something wrong here,' he said. 'There was no obvious reason for the pilot to have engaged the drive. Find out why it did it. Not here,' he said as she leaned forward. 'Do it in the computer room. And do it well,' he added. 'I want to be sure we can trust that thing.'

'How far can I go?' She looked worried. 'I can run a series of checks,' she explained. 'They may give the answer. If

they don't I may have to start disman-
tling. Will you permit that?'

'I can't,' he said. 'I daren't. Do the best
you can without upsetting the function of
the ship. We may have to move and move
fast. I want to be ready to do that in case
of need.'

'Holmson?'

'Yes. He found something down there,'
said Easton. 'Something which threw him
off-balance. It could have been a settlement of some kind. Something alien to
the planet.'

'They could have spotted him,' she
said. 'Shot him down, perhaps.'

'That's right.' He stared sombrely at
the screens. 'And, if they did that, they
could have sent something against us. I
didn't see it. The instruments didn't
register it. The pilot may have detected it
or, again, there may have been nothing to
detect. That's why I want you to check it
out. I want to be sure.'

'Yes,' she said. Then. 'Is something
wrong? You keep looking at the screens.'

'Something is very wrong.' He caught
her by the shoulders, turned her to face

the screens. 'Look at them. You saw them before. Is there any difference?'

'The planet looks smaller,' she said slowly. 'At least I think it does. And the moon isn't where it was.' She thought she knew the reason. 'We've moved,' she said. 'When we entered M-space we moved.'

'Now look at the sun.'

She looked, saw nothing, shook her head.

'The spots,' he urged. 'I was with Holmson when he checked the primary. There were a couple of big sunspots pretty close to the equator. They aren't there now.' He frowned, thinking about it. 'Have you made contact yet?' he asked Longridge.

'No.'

'He could have crashed,' suggested Adrienne. 'He could be alive and well but with a damaged ship and radio.'

'It's possible,' admitted Easton. 'But I wouldn't like to gamble on it. He saw something, remember. Anyway,' he decided, 'we'll have to go down after him. We've got to find out what's down there.'

'Shall I take down the other auxiliary?'

Longridge was hopeful.

'No. I want you to stay at that radio in case you pick anything up. Try every band. Long wave, medium, short and UHF. VHF too. Scan the entire electromagnetic spectrum.' He looked doubtfully at the controls. 'I want to get the ship back into close-orbit,' he told the girl. 'But that can wait until you've had the chance to do some checking. I'll leave you to it.'

Leaving the control room he dropped down to where the honeycomb rested in frigid isolation. Jud Barman looked up from his work as the captain entered the annex. He was dressed in spotless green and looked annoyed at the interruption. 'You want something?'

'Where's Celia?' He nodded as the woman came from an inner compartment. 'How long will it take to rouse twenty men from the honeycomb?'

'Is there something wrong?'

'We've lost Holmson,' explained Easton. 'I want to send after him. How long?'

'I'm not sure,' she said. 'That's more in Jud's department than mine.'

'Two hours for resurrection and say

another eight for orientation and restoration. They won't be at optimum efficiency,' warned the biomech. 'Not in that time. They should all be given the chance to eat and sleep before becoming fully operational.'

'I want a trained pilot as the first,' decided Easton. 'For the remainder pick those who went in last. Not the ones we kidnapped,' he qualified. 'I've no time to listen to complaints. Choose those who were willing.' He looked curiously at what the biomech had been working on. A grey-red mass of convoluted tissue rested in a sealed flask of nutrient fluid. Pipes and wires trailed from what he recognized as a brain. 'Michele's?'

'That's right.' Barman looked proudly at what he had done. 'I'm getting results,' he said. 'My theory about the degeneration was correct. The frontal lobes are gone, useless, but the anterior portions respond to stimuli.' He adjusted the controls of the mechanism supplying artificial blood. 'A few more hours and we might have had some interesting results,' he said. 'But never mind. It can wait.

Wrap it up, sweetheart,' he said to the woman. 'We've got some labouring to do.'

★　★　★

The pilot's name was Rodgers. He was a short, compact, alert man with fast reflexes and a tremendous self-confidence. He'd worked as a civilian helijet operator until he'd had a bet with Dolman and lost. His penalty was to enter the honeycomb. He'd paid his bet with cheerful good humour. Now he listened to the recording of Holmson's voice, looked thoughtful at its sudden breaking, then glanced at the captain. 'Nothing since?'

'No.'

Rodgers nodded and hitched at the weapon belt hugging his waist. 'A river winding in a loop,' he said slowly. 'Smoke to the north. A valley to the south. The whole thing beyond a wide lake. I guess it might be possible to locate the area — given a hell of a lot of luck.'

'You don't think it possible?'

'How many square miles are down

there?' Rodgers jerked his head to where the planet shone in the screens. 'The visibility is low. I guess you could almost spend a lifetime trying or you could be lucky on the first go. Let's hear that tape again.'

He listened to it five times. He had a long talk with Longridge and did some careful checking of the flight-monitor records. He had a session with Adrienne during which they discussed weight-speed ratios, probabilities, impossibilities and, more important, the approximate latitude Holmson had followed before diving beneath the clouds. She had seen him traverse the planet and had a near-eidetic memory. It had to be enough.

'I'm taking ten men,' he told Easton. 'All armed and as fit as they can hope to be.'

'Take twenty,' suggested the captain.

Rodgers shook his head. 'Ten will be enough. More and I'll lose mobility. I'll hit the planet at the same time Holmson did. I'll follow his flight-pattern the best I can but I'm telling you that it's a thin chance. All I can do is look. If I find anything I'll stay clear and let you know. If I find the site Holmson spoke about I'll leave you to decide. When can I leave?'

'When you're ready,' said Easton. They were still far from the original orbit but Rodgers could be guided to the approximate location. He held out his hand. 'Take it easy,' he said. 'And good luck.'

'Thanks.' Rodgers's grip was firm. 'Don't worry too much,' he said. 'It's my neck, remember?'

They watched him leave on the screens, Longridge at the radio, Adrienne watching while she spoke of something else. 'The pilot,' she said. 'I've run a series of tests. As far as I can discover it is functioning perfectly.'

'Did it say why it engaged the drive?'

'It said that it detected an approaching object of tremendous mass. I know,' she said before he could object. 'We didn't see anything like that and the independent instruments didn't register. But that is what it says.'

'Could it be lying?'

'Impossible.'

'Mistaken, then? Malfunctioning? Damn it,' he exploded. 'There must be some logical answer.'

'I can think of at least two,' she said evenly. 'The first is that the pilot genuinely detected something which would have endangered the ship and took appropriate action. Because of its limited vocabulary it could explain it only by an analogue. The other is that perhaps some outside influence could have caused the same effect. I could do that,' she pointed out. 'It would be a simple matter of tampering with a few circuits.'

'If you knew which were the appropriate circuits,' he reminded. 'It would take an expert to figure them out. There is another explanation,' he said. 'The damn thing could have gone crazy.'

She did not immediately object. 'There is always that possibility,' she admitted slowly. 'Not insanity as we know it, of course, but a derangement caused by a warping or distortion of its components.'

'But it would amount to the same thing?'

'Yes,' she admitted. 'It would.'

Longridge looked up from the radio, the headphones swelling his head into a grotesque, insect-like parody of a human skull. 'Rodgers is about to hit the clouds,' he said. 'Do you want to listen?'

'Put him on,' said Easton. He wasn't surprised that the report sounded almost exactly like that made by Holmson. Crisper, more precise, but much the same. He tensed as the voice grew excited.

'Smoke to the north,' said Rodgers. 'A valley to the south and we've just passed over a wide lake. Can you beat that? We've found the damn place!'

'The river,' said Longridge. 'Look for the river.'

'I've got it. Wide and running in a wide loop. No sign of any settlement though.'

'Look again,' said Easton. 'Tell him to quarter the area,' he said to Longridge. 'Tell him to be certain.'

'Damn it, I am certain,' said Rodgers. 'A valley to the south. A range of low mountains to the north. Thin smoke in that direction.' He sounded faintly puzzled. 'Damn thin. If I wasn't looking for it I'd never have spotted it. Holmson must have had good eyes.'

'Check the river,' said Longridge. 'Is there a clearing?'

'Not a big one. Just thin vegetation but the ground looks right for a landing. Want me to try it?'

'Yes,' said Easton.

'You're going to land?' said Adrienne.

'We haven't much choice,' he said. 'We can land and worry about whoever's down there after we hit the dirt. Or we can stay up here until we find them but the ship isn't armed and we'd be a sitting duck. Or,' he added slowly, 'we can move on and try somewhere else.'

'With a pilot you don't trust and a drive you know hardly anything about?'

'That's the point,' he admitted. 'Another is that double-world systems like this are rare. We know that to get the essential attenuation of atmosphere, any planet we hope to live on must have a moon.'

'Then there isn't any choice,' she said. 'We land.'

He nodded and spoke to Longridge. 'Have Rodgers set out the guide-beacons. Get him to check the area and then come back up here. Alone. I want to send down a strong advance party before risking the ship.'

Rodgers was grinning when he returned despite the blood on his face and the bruises on his body. 'I didn't want to waste any time,' he explained. 'So I piled on the gravities.'

'What's it like down there?' Longridge was impatient for detail.

Rodgers shrugged. 'Just about what you'd guess. The landing area is covered with something like grass. The foothills support bushes. Beyond the clearing are trees, vines, stuff like that. We didn't get too close but it looked harmless enough. No game, of course, the sound of our blast would have driven them away. And no sign of any other kind of life either.'

'Maybe it hasn't shown up yet?'

'Could be,' said Rodgers casually. 'If it does the men I left down there will spot it. They've got a radio so they can tell us if it arrives. They've got guns too,' he added. 'And they know how to use them.' He looked at Easton. 'What's the programme from now on, captain?'

'You go back down. Take a full complement and make sure they're well armed.'

'When do I leave?'

'As soon as I've checked with Doris. In the meantime you'd better get the doctor to look you over.'

'I'm all right.'

'Maybe,' said Easton dryly. 'But do it all the same. She's a very attractive woman,' he added. 'You won't find it an ordeal.'

Doris was busy with her chemicals when he looked into her laboratory. She was flushed, smiling and radiated contentment. Trebor is good for her, thought Easton. And she is good for him. They both show it. 'How much longer?' he asked.

'Not long. Come in and wait. The air's clear,' she said after a while. 'We can breathe it. You know that already,' she admitted, 'but it won't rot our lungs or anything like that. In fact it's a lot cleaner than the smog I used to breathe back home. A little high in water-content, a little rich in carbon-dioxide, the usual trace elements and a fairly high concentration of ozone. Call it what we used to breathe back in the dinosaur age and you won't be far wrong.'

'We didn't breathe it,' he reminded. 'We weren't around then.'

'All right,' she said. 'So I'm out a few years.'

'Any harmful pollens, spores, bacteria?'

'None that I could see but I'm a chemist not a bacteriologist. The air won't kill us, that's the main thing.'

He nodded, then smiled. 'You'd better tell Fred to break out that champagne he's made. This is the time to drink it.'

'We're landing?'

'As soon as the advance party gets settled.'

'Then we'll wait until we hit dirt,' she decided. 'We'll make it a double celebration. We're going to get married,' she explained. 'We want to be the very first.'

111

'That's nice,' he said, and meant it.

'Why don't you join us?' she said pointedly. 'Make it a double ceremony?'

He didn't answer.

'Adrienne is crazy about you,' she said. 'And you're the same about her. You'd know it too if only you'd take time off from worrying about the ship. Well,' she said, 'you won't have to worry much longer. Once we land on Eden you can start beginning to live.'

'Eden?'

'The planet,' she said. 'The new world. It's got to have a name so why not Eden. It's a nice name,' she said seriously. 'Symbolic. You've no objection?'

No, he thought tiredly, I've no objection. Call the damn thing what you like for all I care. Just let's get the ship down in one piece. Let's get settled and started on the real job. Who cares about a name? He felt depressed and wondered why. Maybe it's because I'm bushed, he told himself. I've been living on my nerves for too long now. Or, he thought, is it something else? The journey's nearly over. I'm about to quit my command.

I'm practically right back where I started.

'You don't mind about the name?' she insisted.

'No,' he said. 'It's a good name.'

6

The axe sliced through the air, the blade hitting with a dull *thunk*, a scrap of wood flying from the bole of the tree. Steadily Pete Simpson cut deeper, muscles knotting beneath his white, sweat-shining skin. He was naked to the waist but the excessive humidity gave his perspiration no chance to evaporate. He dropped the axe and stepped back, mopping his face, scowling at the sap-oozing gash he had made. The sap was yellow, the wood pink and remarkably tough. It was, he thought, a damn funny kind of a tree. But, on Eden, a lot of things had turned out to be odd.

'You had enough, Pete?' Jake Elman shifted his rifle from the crook of his right arm. 'You want that I should spell you for a while?'

'Frank'll take over.'

'What's the hurry?' Frank Arnold, the third member of the three-man team, lifted himself on one elbow from where he sprawled beside the big, cross-cut saw. 'The way you talk you'd think we were on piece-work or something. To hell with it. What's one tree more or less?'

'Easton won't like it,' said Jake anxiously. 'We've got a schedule and he wants us to keep to it.'

'To hell with Easton,' said Arnold flatly. 'If he's in that much of a hurry he can blister his own hands.' He looked at the callouses on his palms. 'I didn't ask to come here,' he said. 'And I didn't ask to cut down no damn trees either.'

'We've got to clear the land for planting,' said Jake. 'And we need the wood for other things. That makes sense, don't it?'

'What's the matter with you?' Arnold sat upright, a big, irritable man with sharp blue eyes. 'You like being kidnapped and forced to work on some new planet?'

'I didn't say that,' said Pete. 'But we're here and we may as well make the best of it.'

'Some best!' Arnold rose to his feet.

'Listen,' he demanded. 'We're on a work-detail, right? We're always on a work-detail. Us and all the rest who were snatched. Digging, hauling, cutting down trees. Sweat-work all the time. All right.' He drew a deep breath. 'Why us? Why don't some of the others get blisters on their hands?'

'They do,' said Jake. 'Some of them. Easton explained all that,' he reminded. 'Most of the others are specialists. They're too busy to give us a hand.'

'And you swallow that?' Arnold kicked viciously at the saw. It gave a thin, dying whine. 'The way I see it,' he said, 'is that we were snatched to do the hard work. We can keep on doing it. Us and our kids if we ever have any. Maybe you like that idea. I don't.'

'You can't be sure about that,' said Pete slowly.

'I'm satisfied that's the way things are,' said Arnold. 'And so are most of the others. Well, it isn't good enough. Are you willing to do something about it?'

'Take it easy,' said Jake anxiously. He stepped forward, his rifle hanging by its sling from his left arm. 'You're talking mutiny.'

'I'm talking about making things straight,' snapped Arnold. 'We didn't ask to come here. We were snatched. Well, by God, that's something Easton's got to pay for!'

'Yes,' said Pete thickly. He looked down at his hands. 'I had a girl,' he said. 'We were going to be married. I didn't want to come on the ship.'

'You're a big man,' said Arnold. 'Too big to let Easton get away with it.'

'Don't listen to him,' said Jake. 'He's trying to needle you, Pete. Can't you see that?'

'Shut your mouth,' said Arnold.

'Go up against the captain and you'll get yourself killed,' said Jake. 'What else can he do? He can't take you back home. He can't let you take over. We've got no jails. What else can he do but have you shot?'

'Maybe he'll be the one who gets shot,' said Arnold meaningly. 'He — ' He broke off, turning as something rustled to one side, half-thinking that maybe the captain had sneaked up on them, frowning as he stared into the forest. The thick boles of the trees made the light dim, deceptive, casting pools of shadow among the sparse undergrowth. He caught a hint of movement and felt his mouth go suddenly dry. 'Jake,' he croaked. 'Jake, you've got the gun.' Then, 'Jesus!'

It was about five feet tall, shaped something like a wallaby with a strong tail balancing a squat body on powerful back legs. The upper legs were long, ending in splayed hands equipped with razor-edged talons. The head was mostly like crocodile-jaws and fanged like those of a dog. The cranium was small, the ruby eyes deeply recessed, the skin a dirty green like mouldering leather faintly marked with the pattern of scales. It bounded ten feet forward at a single hop.

'Jake!' Arnold fell back, tripped over the saw, rolled frantically to one side. 'The gun, Jake! Use the gun!'

Jake grabbed awkwardly at the rifle, lifting it to his shoulder just as the thing hopped forward again. A clawed rear foot lashed out and tore the entrails from his body. It turned, the sweep of its tail splintering Arnold's ribs and perforating his lungs. Pete made a desperate snatch at the axe.

The thing hopped forward, kicking as it came.

Pete jerked to one side, felt skin being ripped from his hip and swung the axe with all his strength. The blade missed the skull, biting instead into the shoulder. He ripped it out and sprang into the air as the thick tail lashed at his legs. Again he struck, this time severing one of the upper legs. The thing opened its mouth and hissed. A vile stench filled the air. It kicked again, the claws ripping his pants and leaving savage grooves down his thigh. Swinging the axe he struck with the full power of back and shoulder muscles. He felt the shock as it bit into the flat, sloping skull, his stomach heaving as he smelt the odour of its breath. A pulp of grey and blue oozed from the wound. Releasing the axe he dived to where the rifle lay smeared with blood from Jake's body. Snatching it up he fired and kept on firing until the magazine was empty.

'A hundred and ten pounds,' said Jud Barman. 'Earth weight, that is. Here it's a hundred and thirty.' He turned from the dissecting table which had been set up in one of the huts. Against the raw timber his equipment stood in sharp contrast, stainless steel and gleaming plastic stood on a floor of tamped dirt or on wooden stands. 'It's a well-designed beast. A mass of bone and muscle with a brain about equal to that of a dog. If anything it's a little more convoluted.'

'Which means that it could be that much more intelligent,' said Easton.

'It could be,' admitted the biomech. He stepped to a tap, washed his gloved hands, dried them and stripped off the gloves. 'The blood-base is haemocyanin, that's why it's blue. The concentration is fantastic, the thing is lousy with copper mostly gathered in the skeletal structure with a fair proportion in the major organs. It has two stomachs and seems to favour rock as a digestive medium. One of the stomachs was full of it together with fragments of vegetation and animal tissue. It is basically carnivorous but can get along on vegetation if it has to. The teeth are like those of a bear. The claws and talons are retractable and as sharp as hell. Poisoned, too.'

Nice, thought Easton. Damn nice. Just the sort of creature we could do without. He looked at Barman. 'Can we eat it?'

'Not unless we get the copper out of it first. It wouldn't be worth the trouble.'

Easton looked thoughtfully at the dissected remains. The heart, lungs, and liver looked as he thought they should. The brain, what there was of it, was just a brain. The bones, strongly purple, were just bones. The skin, he thought, should make a pretty tough leather if it could be tanned. Just a collection of organic pieces, he told himself. Still more specimens to add to the butcher's shop that was Barman's workroom. But these particular ones were unique. They had killed two men, or was it three? 'How is Simpson?'

Barman shrugged. 'He was dying when they brought him in,' he said. 'I told you the claws were poisonous. Celia pumped him full of antibiotics but it was a waste of time.' He leaned against the edge of the table and prodded at the remains. 'I'm worried,' he said. 'This thing is never a forest dweller. It needs space to move around in and the contents of the stomach show that it lives on rocky ground. Normally, that is. It could be on the move.'

'Migrating? Moving to breeding grounds? Foraging?'

'I don't know,' admitted the biomech. 'But it wouldn't move into the forest to breed. It's oviparous, an egg-layer.'

'Foraging then?' Easton was insistent.

'Maybe.' Barman frowned. 'I'm thinking of the bison,' he said. 'The old North American buffalo. They used to migrate from Canada all the way down to Texas. Suppose a bunch of aliens had decided to settle on their feeding grounds? They wouldn't have known about the buffalo — not until, one day, they found themselves overrun by a few million of them.'

'The buffalo followed their food supply,' said Easton sharply. 'These things, you say, need rock. That means they'll keep to the mountains, the foothills, the high, stony ground. There's a river and forest to the south of us. The mountains are to the north. There's no apparent reason why they should come down here. It's possible that this one could have been a stray.'

'It's possible,' agreed Barman. 'On this damn planet anything is possible. We just don't know enough about it. But we know one thing,' he added. 'And it's serious. Let me show you.'

The rats were small, naked, a score of them pressed close around their mother who glared at the two men with bright, watchful eyes. The rat and her offspring were in a sealed glass case from which pipes ran to a whispering machine.

'Sometimes,' said Barman musingly, 'I wonder what medical science would have done without the rat. Quick to breed, a litter every two months and a gestation period of from twenty to twenty-five days, they are so close, biologically speaking, to mankind that they make the perfect analogue. What affects them will, almost invariably, affect us.'

'Get on with it,' said Easton impatiently.

'I can do without the lecture.'

'This case contains the control,' said Barman. 'I've kept them in a sterilized atmosphere and they're bred according to plan.' He moved to where a second case stood on a bench. It was devoid of pipes and had a wire-mesh top. It was empty.

Easton stared at it.

'This contained the rats which were exposed to the natural atmosphere and allowed to give birth in that atmosphere. I began experimenting within a week of landing. That was close to three months ago, time for three litters.'

'What happened?'

'They died,' said Barman flatly. 'There's something in the air. I don't know what it is but my guess is that it must be a virus of some kind. It affects both the mother and her offspring. The results are similar to puerperal fever. The death-rate is one hundred per cent.'

★ ★ ★

They had worked hard since they landed, felling trees during the day, ripping them into planks, building huts, sheds, work-shops and living quarters during the floodlit night. Ground had been cleared and seed planted. Already the green tips of potential crops stood high in the alien soil. Power flowed from the ship's reactors to charge the batteries of agricultural machines and trucks, to drive the motors of the saw mill, to send light and energy to the settlement. But there was still a lot to be done.

A hell of a lot, thought Easton as he walked from Barman's workroom. Hydro-ponic tanks had to be built and planted in case the soil-grown crops should turn out to be inedible or the seeds inviable. Or to replace the seed in case of accident. Mapping had to be continued and prospecting carried out to ensure a supply of metals. Tanks had to be constructed for the making of plastics. Tools had to be fashioned, the ecology studied, the natural resources of this new world explored. Oil had to be found, factories established, machine tools manufactured. There had to be a sewage system, a constant water supply, telephone and lighting services installed. Houses had to be built and shops and schools . . .

Schools?

What the hell was the good of schools if there were no children?

What was the good of all the effort if there would be no posterity?

He frowned, fighting a sudden depression as if it were a physical enemy. Another problem, he thought. Two of them in fact. More to add to all the rest. He grappled with them as he walked towards the ship. So the rats had died, well, so what? Men aren't rats, he told himself. Maybe the virus or whatever it was wouldn't attack women. Maybe Barman and Forrest would be able to isolate the destructive factor and find a defence. And, he reminded himself, there is always a way out. We can build sealed huts, he thought. Sterilize the air so as to let the women have their children in safety. We can even use the ship as a lying-in ward. In the meantime oral contraceptives would continue to be issued with the evening meal.

Damn it, he thought with sudden fury.

I'm not going to let this planet beat me. Not now. Not after coming so far, doing so much. And those animals, the hoppers, I can take care of them too.

'I want you to reorganize the work-schedule,' he told Adrienne. 'I want as many men as can be spared to build defences for the settlement. Put Chris Webb in charge of the project. He's a good man with military experience. He'll know what to do.'

She looked at him, not answering.

'You don't like the idea?'

'Chris Webb wasn't a volunteer,' she reminded. 'He could be nursing a grudge.'

'That's why I'm putting him in charge of our defences,' said Easton. 'That and the fact that he's the best man for the job. I want him to feel that he is an important part of things,' he explained. 'I've heard the rumours. A lot of those we snatched think that I regard them as something inferior. As expendable. Give Webb this job and they'll know different. They'll know that I'm entrusting them with the safety of the settlement. With my own life, in fact. With all our lives.'

'Aren't you exaggerating a little?'

'I don't think so. One hopper killed three of our men,' he reminded. 'It had to be chopped and shot to death. Multiply it by a hundred, a thousand, and what then?'

'We'd be overrun,' she admitted.

'Exactly. Give Webb all the help you can. Arrange the change of work-schedule right away. He can use plenty of mechanical aid. Floodlights too. I want a round-the-clock working period. And prepare a rota for a continuous guard.'

'You really are taking this thing seriously,' she said. 'One animal and three dead men and you are turning the schedule upside down.'

'What do you mean?'

'I was wondering if, perhaps, you were using it as a means to divert attention.' She looked at him, her eyes enigmatic. He fought a sudden anger.

'No,' he said shortly. 'I'm not doing it for that.'

★   ★   ★

The brain was as he remembered it, a convoluted mass of tissue in a jar, fed with artificial blood, stimulated into a semblance of life by electrodes buried in the tissue. It was hard to think of it as having once been human. Harder still to remember the friendly shape it had worn. 'Why?' demanded Easton. 'Why is Barman keeping it?'

'For the same reason.' Celia Forrest didn't look at the captain. 'For the information it has buried in its memory. The information on the drive.'

'We've landed,' he said. 'We don't need the drive now.'

'We need all the information we can possibly get,' she corrected. 'On the drive and everything else.'

He looked at her, then at the apparatus gleaming with its sterile perfection. He sensed that the woman was lying. 'There's another reason,' he said. 'What is it?'

'Why don't you ask Barman?'

'I'm asking you.' He reached out, caught her by the arm, stared into her face. 'What is it?' he asked gently. 'Are you in love with Barman and loyal because of that? Do you share his disregard for human emotion? Does experiment, for its own sake, appeal to you so much?'

'Please!' She fought against the pressure of his hand. Coldly he tightened his fingers.

'That's an old man in there,' he said. 'A man who dedicated his life to humanity. Professor Michele — you remember him?'

'I haven't forgotten.' She looked down at his hand. The knuckles showed white in the cold light of the compartment. Beyond the open door stood the empty cells of the honeycomb. The pump feeding the brain made a soft whispering, little louder than a sigh. 'You gave permission,' she reminded. 'You told Barman to go ahead. You said that he could work on Michele's brain.'

'For a reason.' He saw her expression and released his grip. 'I was worried about the ship. The drive was acting oddly. I needed any help I could get.'

'You still need help,' she said. 'We all do.'

'And this can provide it?' He looked at the jar and what it contained. The compartment was cold with the eddying currents of chill from the honeycomb, the liquid helium circulating around the cells. 'How?'

'Jud can tell you that.'

'You tell me.' He looked up, met her eyes. 'I know Jud,' he said. 'I've heard some of his theories. He's a damn good biomech but he has some unusual ideas. He might want to save this brain, for example. This and any others he might get. Yours, mine, it would make no difference. Can you guess why?'

She didn't answer.

'He wrote a paper once,' said Easton. 'It was while he was consultant biomech at the Mayo Clinic. *The use of organic components in mechanical systems.*' It was a damn good paper but it got him kicked out of the clinic and onto the black list of every decent hospital. In it he advocated the use of human brains as computers in robotic systems. Rumour had it that he actually had tested his theories in practice. He might be thinking

131

that, on Eden, he would have a free hand.'

'We're short of labour,' she said. 'You know that, as yet, any woman giving birth will die together with her children. You — '

'We can beat that problem,' he snapped.

'By sterilized environments in which they can have their children?' She had anticipated him. 'What solution is that? Can we colonize this planet that way?'

'We'll find an answer,' he said. 'We have to.'

'When?' She didn't wait for an answer. 'Even if we do it takes eighteen years for a child to grow to maturity. Even with the use of gonadotrophin to ensure multiple births we shall still be short of labour. Why not use the resources of modern medical science to save what we can? What can be so wrong about using the parts of a dead organism?'

'Nothing,' he agreed. 'But would a usable brain be dead? Can you be certain that it wouldn't retain its personality? Would you like to be alive and aware, locked in a plastic case, deaf, blind, dumb, without feeling but otherwise fully conscious? Can you imagine what kind of hell that would be?'

'I hadn't thought,' she stammered.

'No,' he said. 'I didn't either. Not until now.'

'Barman — '

'Jud's full of ideas,' said Easton. 'He probably means well but he forgets one thing. The dignity of mankind. A brain isn't just a handful of tissue to be used in a machine. It isn't a computer. It's a person with all that that implies. Kill it, yes. Torture it, no. Try and understand,' he said. 'We're trying to build something new here. We don't want to carry the old prejudices of the past. We don't want to bind ourselves with old superstitions but, equally so, we don't want to throw all we've learned overboard. A man has got to be important. He has got to be respected until he does something to lose that respect. And science is like a company — it has no soul. I know that Jud hopes to found a scientific technocracy. He isn't going to do it. And one other thing,' he added. 'How do you think the others would feel if they thought that, if they died, they'd wind up a slave in a jar?'

'I don't know,' she said. 'But I can guess.'

'Yes,' said Easton. 'It isn't that hard.' He looked at the brain. 'Kill it,' he ordered. 'Let it die.'

'But — '

'Kill it!' He looked at her. 'You don't want to do it?'

'Barman — '

'To hell with Barman!' He stepped forward, found the switch, threw it and waited until the whisper of the pump had faded to silence. 'There,' he said to the doctor. 'It was as simple as that.'

A giant hand shook the vessel.

The compartment swayed, glass shattering as it fell, the floor tilting to hurl him to one side so that he fell heavily against the wall. He climbed to his feet as a second tremor gripped the ship.

'Earthquake!' Celia was screaming, memories of a childhood spent in the Persian disaster colouring her reaction. She screamed again as, from far below, a deep, continuous rumbling echoed through the vessel. Then it was over. The subterranean rumbling died. The trembling of the ship ceased. Her screams were the only sound.

'All right,' said Easton. He shook the woman. 'It's all right,' he repeated. 'It's over, damn you. It's all over!'

7

Williams, the geologist, was optimistic. 'It could have been an isolated incident,' he said. 'Plenty of areas get a tremor or two and it doesn't mean a thing. The earth isn't as stable as most people like to think.'

'This isn't the earth,' said Easton impatiently. 'It's a new planet. What I've got to know is simple. Are we in a danger zone? Have we landed on a geologically unstable area?'

'I don't know,' admitted Williams. He was a thin, precise man with a thin, precise manner of speaking. 'There's no way I can tell with the limited information at my disposal. I'd need to drill sample cores from over a wide area in order to determine the nature of the underlying rock. The samples, coupled with sonic probes, would give me a good idea as to the nature of the region. But even then,' he added cautiously, 'I couldn't be absolutely certain.'

Certainty, thought Easton dryly. The one thing no man can ever really have. He leaned back, looking at the others. He'd called the council to meet in one of the huts and they lounged around the table, faces limned by the light of a naked bulb. They all showed signs of fatigue. Since the quake everyone had been working non-stop to repair the damage. It could have been a lot worse.

'Listen to the man,' said Longridge. 'He talks like a lawyer.'

'Shut up,' said Barman evenly. 'Every man to his trade.' He looked at Easton and the captain wondered if he knew what he had done. Probably not, he thought. Celia could have blamed the pump-failure on the quake. She would avoid trouble if it was possible. 'All right, captain,' said the biomech. 'You're the boss. You call it.'

'Call what?' said Trebor. 'There's nothing to call.' He glared at the geologist. 'Hell man, can't you even make an educated guess?'

'No.' Williams was stubborn. 'We've

had a couple of minor tremors,' he pointed out. 'We may never get another or, if we do, it may not be for years. Think of Japan and California,' he urged. 'They are both in an earthquake area yet how often does disaster strike?'

'In other words we're back where we started from,' said Longridge. 'We just don't know. Well, so much for expert advice.' He looked at Easton. 'It seems to boil down to a simple matter of choice. We either stay here or move somewhere else. Do we vote on it?'

Easton nodded. 'Fred?'

'I vote we stay.' Trebor was emphatic. 'The crops are coming along nicely,' he said. 'Doris has checked the local environment and we know how we stand with regard to supplementing the local growth-elements. If we move we'll have it all to do over again.'

'That's no problem,' said Barman. 'We can live on the ship if we have to. A few months more on yeast won't kill us.'

'You vote we move?' said Easton.

'Yes.'

'Longridge?'

'If we're thinking of the future this is the place to be,' said the engineer. 'Plenty of mineral deposits and torrents in the mountains for hydro-electric installations if and when we need them. I vote that we stay.'

'How about you, Chris?'

'I've sweated blood over those defences,' said Webb feelingly. He was a blond giant of a man who had gladly accepted responsibility. 'They're operational now but, if we move, I can't guarantee to protect the ship.'

'You vote we stay then?'

'I do.'

'Then it's decided,' said Easton. 'We stay.' He leaned back, closing his eyes, conscious of a minute lessening of responsibility. So this is what democracy is all about, he thought. It isn't a government of the majority, it's a way to duck out from under in case of need. Get them talking, he told himself. Then get them to vote. The majority decide — but who picks those to vote to start with and who can tell if the vote isn't rigged or not? As it was in this case. As I knew it would be. He opened his eyes at the sound of Barman's voice.

'Talking of defences,' he said casually. 'How many men have we lost to date?'

'Thirteen.' Webb was curt.

'All killed by hoppers?'

'All but two — they died by accident. They got crushed by falling trees,' said Webb impatiently. 'I reported the matter to the captain.'

'Did he tell you to dispose of them?'

'No. I had them buried.'

'I see.' Barman straightened in his chair. 'Why didn't you bring them to me? How else am I supposed to find an antidote for the hopper poison?'

'You have dead hoppers and you have rats,' said Webb. 'You can play with them.'

'Play?'

'Call it what you like.' Webb was defiant. 'Listen,' he said. 'You're a biomech and your kind is just getting into its stride back home. Spare parts for the rich. I know all about it. Well, that's back home. We can do without your breed here.'

'Can you?' Barman's voice was very

soft. 'You stupid, primitive, unthinking ape,' he said cuttingly. 'Wait until you lose an eye — then you'll scream for my 'breed' fast enough. And from where am I supposed to get a replacement eye? Or a heart, a kidney, a spleen? Those dead men could have helped stock the tissue banks. Tell him,' he said to Easton. 'Give him the order. All dead men are to be brought to me. All of them. There are to be no more secret burials.'

'Ghoul!' said Webb.

'He's right.' Easton commanded their attention. 'We can't afford waste,' he said quietly. 'An injured man is a liability. A crippled man the same. You will do as Barman says. The dead are his responsibility. But the brains,' he said looking at the biomech, 'will be destroyed. All of them.'

It was one matter he didn't intend putting to the vote.

★ ★ ★

Adrienne was busy in the computer room. She looked up as Doris entered, a

141

crease between her eyes, her red hair showing need of attention. The chemist looked at her then shook her head. 'For a girl who is chasing a man,' she said. 'You certainly aren't trying.'

'Don't be a fool!'

'Why say that? Have you opted out of the human race?'

'I'm busy,' snapped Adrienne. 'What do you want?'

'The chance to talk to another woman.' Doris deliberately took a seat. 'Knock off for ten minutes,' she suggested. 'The world will last that long.'

'Look,' said Adrienne tensely. 'You may have nothing to do but I have. Now why don't you go away and let me get on with it?'

'Get on with what? Talking to your boy friend?' Doris nodded towards the computer. 'That's what that thing has become, you know. You're never around. You never go anywhere, talk to anyone. You spend all your time cooped up in here talking to our ex-pilot. Do you think that's the smart way to catch yourself a man?'

'I don't want a man.'

'You're a liar,' said Doris calmly. 'Every woman who is a woman wants a man. And I know the man you want. Why don't you do something about it?'

'Why don't you mind your own business?'

'This is my business. I'm not worried so much about you,' confessed Doris. 'It's the captain I'm thinking about. Have you seen him lately? Call him a bundle of nerves and you'd be flattering. The man's eaten up with worry. Damn it, Adrienne! Even you know that all work and no play is the short route to a nervous breakdown. Why don't you give him a break?'

'Listen,' said Adrienne tightly. 'In the first place you don't know what you're talking about. In the second place you're about as wrong as you can be. And in the third place — ' She broke off, unable to mention that time during the trip when she'd had his door closed in her face. Never again, she told herself. Once is enough to be made to feel like dirt. To be rejected. To have what you offer thrown back in your face. I wouldn't do it again if his life depended on it. Or my life. 'Forget it,' she said. 'Forget the whole thing. Be satisfied with the happiness you have without trying to give it to everyone else.'

'I am happy,' admitted Doris. 'Happier than I've ever been before. Fred's a good man.'

Adrienne didn't comment.

'All right,' said Doris. 'I've said what I came here to say. Now let's talk about something else.' She looked at the panel of the computer. 'What's old tin-head got to say that's interesting?'

'Quite a lot.' Adrienne accepted the change of subject at its face value. 'I've been running some checks,' she explained. 'Analogues of probable situations so as to determine their logical outcome. Some of the results aren't very encouraging.'

'Such as?'

'The supply of oral contraceptives can't last forever. Can you make more?'

'Sure. Given the equipment and the time.'

'And if you should die?'

'Why should I die?'

'You could be killed by accident, a

144

hopper, anything. Let's assume that you are. What then?'

'I'm not so sure,' said Doris slowly. 'We're pretty short on chemists with the necessary technical knowhow to do the job.'

'If you should die before you make more of the contraceptives and before you can train someone else to do it,' said Adrienne. 'And with things as they are now. The last woman will die in childbirth within twelve years. That is assuming that all are fertile.'

'But we can take precautions! The ship — '

'The ship will be uninhabitable within six,' said Adrienne. 'You've forgotten that it is a delicate mechanism with a carefully balanced life-support system. No matter how careful we are the external atmosphere will penetrate and contaminate the interior. The air-sterilizing system will be unable to carry the load. Would you like another forecast?'

'Why not?' said Doris. The little bitch is trying to frighten me, she thought. Getting her own back for me having told her the truth. 'Let's hear the worst.'

'Let us assume that the crops prove inedible,' said Adrienne. 'If we all have to continue to live off the ship we shall be starving within four years.'

'The yeast tanks need sugar,' admitted Doris. 'If we can't supply it then the yeast will starve and die. But we can use algae,' she said. 'That only needs sunlight and air.'

'True,' said Adrienne. 'If the algae continue to breed true. I am assuming that it will not.'

'You're stacking the cards your way,' protested Doris. 'If you do that you can make the answers come out just how you want. That isn't a genuine analogue.' She frowned, thinking. 'Try this for size,' she suggested. 'On the basis of all available data what are the chances of the colony being a success?'

Adrienne transmitted the instructions. The answer was almost immediate.

'In reply to your question,' said the computer with its mechanical voice. 'The answer is that the colony does not stand any chances at all of being a success.'

'You're lying!' Doris stared at the girl. 'You fixed it,' she accused. 'You're trying to scare me.'

'No.' Adrienne was contemptuous. 'You phrased the question,' she reminded. 'You said, 'on the basis of all available data'. The temperature of this region has increased by twenty per cent since we landed. On the basis of such an increase it is obvious that no living thing could survive here for long. It would grow too hot,' she explained. 'In three years the temperature would be that of boiling water.'

'But this is summer,' said Doris.

'Why? Because of the growth of vegetation? For all we know the growth here could take place in the winter.'

'No.' Doris was positive. 'The days are longer than the nights,' she pointed out. 'This must be summer.'

'Agreed,' said Adrienne. 'But we have no way of telling how long it will last or how hot it will get. Have we?'

'No,' admitted Doris. She's done it, she thought. She's managed to scare me but I'll be damned if I give her the pleasure of knowing it. 'We don't know a lot of things,' she said and managed to smile. 'For all we know this planet could be falling into the sun.'

'Yes,' said Adrienne. She was quite serious. 'It could be. Would you like another example?'

'I'd like the answer to one last question,' said Doris. 'Is it all right if I ask?'

'Go ahead.'

'Just what happened between you and the captain for you to hate his guts?'

'That,' said Adrienne flatly, 'is not an acceptable question.'

'In other words you're telling me to go to hell?'

'Exactly,' said Adrienne.

*   *   *

Fred Trebor left the hut in which he worked among plants, fertilizers and soil samples, crossed the landing field, skirted the recreation ground and paused to watch Chris Webb train some of his guards. The blond had built a small rifle range and was busy teaching five men how to shoot. They were using air rifles firing a 4mm steel ball-bearing and, though the range of the guns was limited, they were accurate for the purpose.

'All right,' yelled Webb. He wore cross belts and carried a holstered pistol. 'Now remember this. It isn't how many shots you fire that's important. It's where you put them. Now load and take position.' He saw Trebor and waved a greeting. 'We'll try some snap shooting,' he told his men. 'Starting from the right I want you to shoot at the target when it appears. I want you to aim and fire in two seconds flat. Ready? Go!' He gestured to an assistant at the end of the range. A silhouette of a hopper, a third life-size, sprang suddenly into view. The man on the extreme right jerked up his rifle and fired. There was a metallic *ping*.

'Good,' commented Webb. 'Nice and fast. Where did he hit?'

'Chest,' called back the assistant. He lowered the target, moved it to one side, let it spring up again. 'Belly!' he called. Then, 'Head! Missed! Belly!'

'Numbers three and four try again.' Webb glared at the two men. 'Don't get flustered and don't try to be clever. The skull of a hopper is almost solid bone. A bullet aimed at the head could be wasted. A bullet that misses should never have been fired. Take enough time, aim low and hit them smack in the guts.' He called to his assistant. 'Keep them at it until I tell you to stop.'

He joined Trebor, standing beside the gardener as he watched the men at their practice. One of them said something and the others laughed. Webb glowered. 'The trouble with some of them,' he complained, 'is that they don't take it seriously.'

'Maybe if you used real guns they would,' suggested Trebor.

'Sure, but what do we use for ammunition?' Webb hooked his thumbs in his weapon-belt. 'Those air guns are the same weight and shape as the one's they'll be using. When they can aim and fire and score a hit every time I'll get them on the real thing. Teach them how to load and clear a blockage. Maybe even let them fire a few rounds to get used to the noise.' He looked at Trebor. 'It'll be your turn soon.'

'Think again,' advised Trebor. 'I'm too busy to play soldiers.'

'I want every man and woman to be able to use a gun,' Webb said grimly. 'The time may come when they'll have to.'

'You're joking.'

'No,' said Webb. 'I'm not joking. You wouldn't be joking either if you'd seen a hopper rip out a man's guts. Those things are about the most vicious form of life I've come across. They don't seem to feel pain. You shoot them and they just keep coming until they drop.' He looked towards the north. 'They live up there somewhere,' he said. 'They come down towards the river. As yet there's only been a few of them, two or three together at the most. They come and we kill them and then there's a wait until we see some more.'

'Strays?'

'Could be. I hope so.'

'You're pessimistic,' said Trebor. 'All soldiers are. They have to be.' He looked at the other man. 'You've been in the army,' he said. 'Right?'

Webb nodded.

'Seen action?'

'I was in Vietnam as a kid. From there I moved to India when the Chinese tried to take over. Then I was in Africa with the U.N.O. until the Congofederation kicked us out. After that I bummed around for a while, joined a bunch in South America, ran a few guns, stuff like that. Finally I joined the project.' He gave a short laugh. 'I was a security guard. How do you like that? I was so good that I couldn't even stop myself from getting snatched.'

'Any hard feelings?'

'Not now,' said Webb. He hitched again at his weaponbelt. 'You people need me,' he explained. 'You're all so damned innocent. Someone's got to look after you.'

'Do the others feel like that? The ones we snatched, I mean?'

Webb shrugged, not answering. Trebor didn't press the matter. Instead he said, 'I'll be throwing a party soon. It's Doris's birthday and I want to celebrate. I'm inviting you to come.'

'A party,' said Webb. He licked his lips. 'With liquor?'

'There'll be plenty to drink,' promised Trebor. 'I've got a batch brewing and it'll be ready for the day. Keep it in mind, uh?'

'Sure,' said Webb. 'I'll do that.'

*   *   *

Trebor moved on, halting at the edge of a patch of standing corn. It looks good, he thought. It looks real good. He tore off one of the swelling ears, stripping the tassels so as to expose the cob. The grain was white, firm and very large. He gouged at it with his thumb and juice spurted over his fingernail. A few more weeks, he told himself. Just a few more weeks and we can set about harvesting this patch at least. He felt elated at the prospect.

Lifting his head he looked at the other patches. They spread from the edges of the landing field to the limits of the cleared area. Wheat, oats, and barley. Sunflowers, rape, and peanuts for seeds,

153

food and oil. Jute, flax, and hemp for fibre. Cane and beets for sugar. He had planted them all in carefully measured areas so as to be able to determine the exact yield. Peas, beans, broccoli, cabbage, potatoes, spinach, onions, swedes . . . a little of everything to see what would happen.

They're working, he thought. Each and every one of them is working all the time, sending down roots, transmuting the energy of the sunlight, building usable materials from air and water and soil. A million chemical processing laboratories within every tiny leaf.

We could live on vegetation alone, he thought. Build a civilization on it. Plants could be bred to extract metals from the ground, copper and arsenic, selenium and iron. They can supply us with oil, fibre, a pharmacopoeia of drugs. We can grow sugar to make into alcohol to drive the agricultural machines. We can grow protein for our diet, dyes for our clothes and, given time, furnishings for our homes.

Why not? he thought. Gourds can be

used as bottles and trees can be trained so that their branches take usable shapes. And we haven't even begun to investigate the field of artificially induced plant-mutation. Of irradiation so as to make transplants of opposed types viable. We could make a tree, he told himself. A tree with hollows which could be used as rooms. Soft moss to line those rooms. Fungi, nuts, and fruit which could be in spore, seed, blossom, and fruit all at the same time. Pods which would yield soporifics and stimulants. Leaves which would give protection and clothing. Spines, even, to ward off potential predators.

We could do it, he thought, and then corrected himself. Not we, I. What do the others know about botany? The most they can do is to stick the seed in the ground and hope. They wouldn't know what to do if the wheat showed red with blight, the barley spotted with ergot. They haven't the knowledge to rotate crops, to know which should follow which and for why. They need me, he told himself. They can't do without me. If they want to damn well eat then they'd better remember that I'm the one who supplies the food.

Hell, he thought gleefully. I'm the most important man on the goddamned planet. Doris should be proud of me!

8

The river was a wide stream of turgid water almost stagnant between low banks shaded by trees. Insects hovered at the water's edge and Longridge slapped mechanically at them as he sat on the bank, his back against the bole of a tree. Beside him a crude fishing rod was stuck at an angle in the soft dirt. Idly he watched the makeshift float bobbing close to the bank.

'You're wasting your time,' said Rodgers. 'You know that?'

'It's my time,' said Longridge.

'You'll never catch anything this close to the bank.' Rodgers sat down beside the engineer. 'Want to bet?'

'I want to fish.'

'Then try further out.'

'Go to hell,' said Longridge pleasantly. He grunted as the float ducked under the water. 'Still want to bet?'

'It could be a false alarm.'

'Not this time.' Longridge grinned as a shiny body broke the surface, wriggling as he swung it through the air towards him. Rodgers twisted aside as it plopped on the grass.

'Careful,' he warned. 'It could be dangerous.'

Together they examined the alien fish. It was the size of a trout with gaudy colouring and a ridge of spines running down its back. As they watched it began to expand, puffing up to five times its original size. It looked a little like a Japanese dragon.

'Defence mechanism,' said Longridge thoughtfully. 'That means that it probably isn't poisonous.'

'It is,' said Rodgers. 'I caught one weeks ago,' he explained. 'Way out in deep water. I didn't recognize this one at first, mine was puffed out when it left the water. I took it to Meldew. The damn things are full of tetrodotoxin. Get stung by one of those spines and you'll die of muscular paralysis.' He watched as Longridge killed the fish with a rock. 'There are other kinds,' he said gloomily.

'One with vestigial legs and another which folds itself into a prickly ball. That one was full of holothurin. Meldew doesn't reckon on us ever having fish on the menu.'

Meldew was the pisciculturalist. He'd built a small boat and trawl and was busy exploring an entire new world of aquatic organisms.

'I'm not worried about eating them,' said Longridge. 'I just want to catch them.'

'Sure,' said Rodgers. He scowled at the dead fish. 'I don't understand this,' he said. 'I caught mine out in deep water. I wonder what made this one come in so close to the bank?'

'Need there be a reason?' Longridge baited his hook with a scrap of flesh. 'Clams,' he explained. 'I found a cluster of them beneath a rock.' He threw out the baited hook. 'Maybe it just came in for food?' he suggested. 'Or maybe it just wanted some shade. It's hot out there.'

'It's hot everywhere,' admitted Rodgers. 'But that wouldn't worry a fish. A bigger fish might, but not the heat.' He stared thoughtfully at the bobbing float then swore as an insect settled on his bare throat. He slapped and examined the remains stuck to his fingers. 'You know,' he said feelingly, 'this damn planet's got it in for us.'

'Could be,' agreed Longridge. He settled back against the tree, resting his weight on his shoulders. 'Look at it this way,' he suggested. 'A planet is a living organism. It has life of its own, sure, but it's a balanced ecology. Then we arrive. We're strangers. Invaders. We settle down and start to spread out. In essence we're exactly like a virulent bacteria invading a healthy organism. So the planet starts to fight back.'

'You're nuts!'

Longridge smiled.

'All right,' said Rodgers. 'I'll play along. So you're drawing an analogy between the planet and us. If we get invaded by bacteria we begin manufacturing antibiotics to beat them off. Is that what you mean?'

Longridge nodded. 'What happens when we get ill? We run a high temperature. We mass leucocytes at the point of infection to contain the enemy. We could even break out in boils.'

'The climate, the hoppers, the earthquake.' Rodgers glared at the engineer. 'You're having me on.'

'It's a theory,' soothed the engineer. 'You don't have to believe it.'

'You're damn right I don't!' snapped the pilot. 'I — ' He broke off at the sound of a high-pitched squeal. 'What the hell?'

'It's some of the women come down to bathe,' said Longridge. 'They use a stretch of water lower down.' He listened to the squeals and splashings. 'Well,' he said gloomily, 'that puts an end to fishing for today. That racket's enough to clear the river.' He lifted the line from the water and unbaited the hook. 'May as well get back to the grindstone,' he said as he wrapped the line around the pole. 'I knew this was too good to last.'

'Much to do?'

'The usual,' said the engineer. 'Lines here, lines there, lines goddam everywhere. I've got help, sure, but there are some things I like to do myself.' He looked curiously at the pilot. 'And you? How come you're taking time off from the job?'

'I'm bushed,' said Rodgers simply. 'I've been on my feet for sixty-five hours and I'm beginning to see double. I ruined three hours work with a slip of a screwdriver and that's enough. The damn helicopter can wait until I've caught up on my sleep.'

'Easton won't like it.'

'I don't like it either,' admitted the pilot. 'But so what? That quake did too much damage for me to put it right with a snap of the fingers. I'm the guy that's going to fly that thing and it's my neck I'm worried about.' He yawned and stretched himself on the grass. 'Not to worry,' he said sleepily. 'A few hours one way or the other can't make all that much difference. Anyway, I'm due for some sack time.' He jerked upright, suddenly fully awake. 'What the hell was that?'

It came again. The scream of women in the extremity of terror.

★ ★ ★

They reached the swimming place at the same time, jerking to a halt as they stared towards the river. Something big threshed the surface in mid-stream.

It was long, scaled, a dirty grey. Gaping jaws revealed triple rows of blue, murderous teeth. From either side of the wide mouth a long, tentacle-like append-age reached forward, the broad tips churning the water. Just ahead of them a woman swam for her life.

She dug her arms into the water, threshing her legs with a desperate need for speed, her milk-white skin soft and vulnerable against the scales of the beast. Most of her companions had reached the bank. A few were still in the water wading to safety. They were the ones who screamed. The woman in the water did not scream — she had no breath to waste.

'For God's sake where's the guard?' Rodgers glared around the area. 'Hasn't anyone got a gun?'

'Over here!' Longridge ran to where clothes were heaped beneath a tree. Two rifles surmounted the pile. 'They're modest,' he panted as he snatched up one of the weapons. 'They don't like men to watch them when they bathe. I guess those who were supposed to stand guard joined in.' He turned, lifting the rifle to his shoulder, aiming at the beast. 'Try and get its eyes.'

He squeezed the trigger and felt the gun kick against his shoulder. Tiny fountains leaped from the water beside the creature. He steadied himself and tried again. This time bluish spots sprang out against the dirty grey of the scales, tiny holes marked with the white of fat, pulsing with purple blood. They looked utterly insignificant. It was, he thought, like pricking an elephant with a pin. He shifted his aim and sent bullets searing into the open mouth. The ugly whine of ricochets echoed across the water. Spray rose as the thing lashed its tail.

Beside him Rodgers cursed as his rifle fell silent, swearing as he fought to clear a jammed cartridge.

'She'll never make it!' Longridge glared at the woman, the tentacles reaching towards her. 'Damn it, man, can't you get into action?'

'I've got it!' Rodgers expelled the defective shell. 'Let's go!'

He ran towards the water, dropped to one knee, sent a stream of bullets towards the creature's snout. Longridge stayed where he was, aiming and firing with cold deliberation, trying to blind the beast, to injure it, to slow it down. Almost he succeeded. The woman reached the shallows, rose to her feet, stumbled towards the bank. Like a whip one of the tentacles reached towards her, knocked her down, jerked her towards the gaping mouth.

The river turned red as the jaws clamped down on her flesh.

'Cover me!'

Rodgers dropped his empty rifle and ran into the water. He gripped the woman by the arm, heaved, flung himself backwards. Longridge fired, holding his aim, sending bullets smashing at the point where the tentacle joined the body. It shredded beneath the repeated blows, fell limp and useless, the junction oozing blood. The creature threshed, turned, and received the last of the bullets down its throat. It backed to mid-stream.

'Help me!' Rodgers was waist-deep in the river supporting the limp form of the woman. Red stained the water around him. He kept both hands below the surface. 'Her leg's gone,' he said. 'Get me something to use as a tourniquet. Hurry!'

Longridge ran to the heap of clothing, snatched up a belt, ran back into the water. He followed the lines of the woman's body, touched the stump, twisted the belt above the wound, burying it deep in the flesh. 'That should do it,' he said. He looked at the pale, unfamiliar face. 'She's unconscious.'

'It's just as well,' said Rodgers.

'Are you all right?'

'Yes. The beast?'

'Dead I think. Or dying.' Longridge stared to where the creature floated in mid-stream. It twitched once then stayed motionless. 'Now we know why that fish came in so close to the bank,' he said. 'That thing must have been out there all the time. Waiting.'

'We'd better get her to the doctors,' said Rodgers.

The fly had a fat red body, blue wings, and a pair of metallic green eyes. It buzzed, hovered a moment, then struck. Charles Pierce swore, slapped viciously at his neck, swore again as the fly buzzed safely away. 'Damn things,' he muttered. 'Why the hell don't they give us some stuff to keep them off of us?'

'Maybe they haven't got it?' suggested his companion. Pierce shook his head.

'They've got it all right,' he grumbled. 'Do you see Webb bitten half to death? Do you see Easton eaten alive? Or Longridge? Or Barman? Or any of the other toffee-nosed slobs? Like hell you do.'

'Knock it off,' said Roy Seegan. 'I'm getting tired of you bitching all the time.'

'You like it here?' said Pierce. 'You like having been snatched and put to work without pay? Without any say so in what you do? You call yourself a man?'

'I'm man enough to shove this rifle down your throat if you don't watch it,' growled Seegan. He was a big man with a thick neck and could probably do what he threatened. Pierce wasn't cowed.

'You could try it,' he admitted. 'I'll give you that. But you wouldn't have the chance to try it twice.' He moved in the rifle pit, letting his weapon fall so that it pointed directly at the other man. 'I could have an accident,' he suggested. 'My finger could slip. I could shoot you down like a dog and I'd get away with it. You still want to shove that rifle down my throat?'

'Quit riding me.' Seegan slapped at his cheek and squashed a fly. It made a wet sound as he hit it and left a stain on his cheek. Irritably he stared at his companion. Pierce was smaller than himself, a runt with the courage of a cornered rat, a man who was dangerous because he was afraid. He would kill if he thought himself threatened. He would kill if he was hurt. He would kill merely to save himself from further injury. And he had a vindictive nature. 'Look,' said Seegan. 'We're here. We might as well make the most of it.'

'The most of what? This?' Pierce gestured towards the cleared area before the rifle pits, the woods beyond, the mountains beyond the woods. 'You want to be a toy soldier all your life? Do this and do that and don't dare to call your soul your own? Hell, if that's all you wanted from life what kept you? You could have enlisted any time back home. They love dopes with brawn and no brain. You might even have made sergeant.'

'Shut up,' said Seegan.

'Make the most of it,' muttered Pierce. 'That's what you said. That's what Pete Simpson said too and where is he now? Dead and under that's where. Frank Arnold now, he had guts.'

'He's dead too,' reminded Seegan.

'Sure, and who put him where he was bound to get it?' Pierce jerked his thumb back at the ship. 'They killed Frank. They killed Pete and Jake and all the rest. They wouldn't have died if they'd been left back home,' he pointed out. 'They were snatched and that makes it murder. Are you going to wait until they get you too?'

Seegan shook his head, irritable at the

flow of disturbing ideas, wishing that Pierce would just shut up or talk about other things. He reminded him of an agitator the union had sent down to the project at one time. He'd had the same way of needling a man so that he didn't know if he was coming or going. The agitator had vanished one dark night. He wondered if Pierce would do the same.

'Do you think they've treated us right?' demanded Pierce. 'Look at the way they've treated you. Aren't you as good as Webb? Did they offer you the job to rule the roost? Did they hell? Damn it, Roy, you could take Webb and break him apart in your bare hands. But the guys like you, they trust you, and they know you wouldn't let them down. Webb has sold us all short.'

Seegan made a grunting sound and his hands closed over the stock of his rifle.

'They got the best of it,' said Pierce. 'They eat good, have a drink now and again, the pick of the girls. They sleep at night while we watch out and get bitten by flies. They look after themselves all along the line and we're the mugs who stand for it. Look,' he added. 'Do you see any of them standing guard night after night? Do you?'

'No,' said Seegan. He swallowed. 'You're right, Charlie,' he said. 'We've been taken. But what can we do about it?'

'Nothing yet,' said Pierce quickly. 'I want to sound out the rest of the boys. If they aren't willing to kick in with us then to hell with them. They can take what's coming. That's fair enough, isn't it, Roy? Do you want to do it all alone?'

'No,' Seegan slapped again at his cheek. 'What's the plan?' he demanded. 'Take over the ship and head back home? Is that it?'

'That's it.' Pierce watched him, his eyes very bright. 'You got a better one?'

Seegan shook his head. 'But can we do it? I mean, can we fly the crate?'

'I'll fix that,' said Pierce. 'You just sit tight and wait for the word. If you get into trouble I'll back you all the way. If they jump on me you do the same. Deal?'

Solemnly they shook hands.

★　★　★

Celia came from the inner room which they now used as a hospital. She closed the door and leaned against it. She looked very tired. 'She's dead,' she said. 'She's just died.'

Barman leaned back in his chair. A microscope stood before him surrounded by an orderly litter of slides. He palmed his eyes, pressing both hands into his orbits, blinking as he took them away.

'She shouldn't have died,' said Celia. 'We bypassed her heart to beat muscular paralysis, kept her sedated to avoid shock, filled her veins with saline, glucose, and antibiotics. But she's dead.'

'Yes,' said Barman. 'She would be.'

'The injury was relatively minor,' protested Celia. 'The loss of a leg from just above the knee. There was some bruising and tearing of tissue, some crushing of bone, hardly any important loss of blood. She was unconscious almost at once and we kept her that way. The wound was ugly, true, but we cleaned up the torn flesh, sutured the veins, arteries, and blood vessels, sewed it close and neat. And yet she died.' The doctor shook her head in bafflement. 'I don't understand why she did.'

'There was infection,' he said curtly. 'You can understand that.'

'We took precautions. And what infection could kill so fast?'

'A poison could,' he reminded. 'But it wasn't a poison which killed her.' He gestured towards the microscope. 'I've taken smears and samples of blood, tissue, and lymph. That girl was as good as dead when they brought her in. Nothing we could have done would have saved her. All we did was simply a waste of time.'

'She should have been taken to the ship. The air is sterile there. She would have been free of air-borne bacteria.'

'It wouldn't have made the slightest difference,' he said patiently. He looked at her with sudden suspicion. 'This girl — she means something to you?'

Yes, she thought dully. She meant something to me. She was the conscience of the past returning to accuse. I killed her, she told herself. I got her ready for the honeycomb. She'd changed her mind and didn't want to come but I tricked her. I knocked her out with a shot of pentathol. I thought I was being clever. I didn't guess that I was condemning her to death.

'I remember her,' she said, coming forward to sit at the table. 'I got her ready for the honeycomb.' She looked at the slides. 'What killed her?'

'Eggs.' He met her stare. 'This planet has some peculiar methods of reproduction,' he explained. 'When she was bitten the teeth of that creature injected a stream of microscopic eggs into her bloodstream. Had events followed their natural course the injection would have had no consequence. She would have been eaten and either digested or regurgitated. From what happened we can assume that she would have been digested.'

'The eggs?'

'I imagine they are a final line of defence,' he said. 'A means to survive no matter what. If the creature is attacked by something stronger and bigger than itself and is vanquished, it can still gain a victory of a kind. Its progeny will develop in the body of the host and eat it from within. All it needs to do is deliver one healthy bite.' He looked at the doctor. 'I imagine,' he said dryly, 'that the creature has few natural enemies.'

'It has more now,' she said. 'Webb is going to run nets across the river and station a guard to blow the things apart with rocket shells.'

'He is also insisting that every man carries arms at all times,' said Barman. 'As if a gun could kill the biggest menace of this planet.'

'The rats?'

'They keep dying. You know that. No matter what I try or do they keep dying.' He led her to the cages which stood against one wall. In the one with piped air a pregnant rat was close to her time. It was obvious that she was far from well. 'I handled her,' he explained. 'Ten days ago I took her out of the cage and exposed her to the natural environment.'

'Ten days,' she said thoughtfully. 'About halfway through gestation. In a woman that would be almost five months.'

'I wanted to find out how close to confinement they could be exposed and still survive,' he explained. 'The answer is no time at all. It bears out the theory that I've been working on. I believe that the virus could attack through the pituitary. Pregnancy disturbs the secretions of that gland as gonadotrophin does. If that is the case nothing but complete isolation will ever enable any woman to bear a living child on Eden.'

There should, she thought, have been a bell somewhere. A big, heavy, deep-voiced bell.

Tolling.

9

The helicopter buzzed in a slow circle around the settlement, the rotors a shimmering blur above the squat cabin, the snarl of its engine strange in the normal, electric silence. It hovered, tilted, drifted gently down to rest. Rodgers jumped down from the cabin and patted the fuselage. 'There's my girl,' he said.

'How did it go?' asked Easton.

'Like a bird.' The pilot wiped the back of his hand across his forehead. His face and hands were stained with ingrained oil and grease, his eyes red with fatigue. 'Like an old and careful bird,' he added. 'But she got me up and kept me up and that's all that matters.'

'Not quite,' said Easton. He looked at the machine. The helicopter had been under cover when the quake had shaken the area and a falling roof had done nothing to improve its appearance. The rotors had been straightened and bright metal showed where replacements had been fitted, but the skin was patched and ragged.

'She'll be all right,' said Rodgers, guessing his thoughts. 'I've put in too much work on her not to be sure of that. I'll take it anywhere you want it to go.'

'And bring it back?'

'What else?' Rodgers squinted at the lowering ceiling of unbroken cloud. It was growing dark and the clouds seemed heavier than usual. 'I'll tell you one thing though. From now on she stays in the open. She can be staked and roped down but that's all.' He rubbed at his face again and scowled at his hands. 'I look a mess,' he said. 'I've got to get cleaned up.'

'Doris won't mind,' said Easton. 'She knows that you've been busy.'

'I mind,' said the pilot. 'Only a bum would turn up at a party looking like a tramp.' He grinned at his own humour. 'Anyway, I could use a bath. Some ice-water and about a ton of detergent would just about get me clean and cool. See you?'

'At the party? Sure.' Easton watched the pilot walk towards the communal bathhouse. He would bathe and maybe sleep for an hour and then seem as refreshed as if he'd had a whole night's sleep. The man had an amazing capacity for punishment. Which, he thought, was just as well. It was a pity that they didn't all share the pilot's stamina.

Longridge emerged from the lower entry port as Easton approached the ship. The engineer looked trim, smart in clean clothing, even the weapon-belt at his waist bearing a high polish. He carried a small parcel beneath one arm.

'How do I look?' he demanded.

'Like a tailor's dummy,' said Easton. He looked curiously at the parcel. 'What's that you've got there?'

'Not much.' Longridge opened the package. It contained a small, crudely carved doll made from the local wood. 'Just something for Doris,' he said. 'For her birthday. Think she'll like it?'

'She'll love it.'

'I hope so.' Longridge rewrapped the doll then eased his belt. 'This damn thing's cutting me in half,' he complained. 'Do we have to wear them all the time?'

'Yes,' said Easton. 'All of us. Webb thinks that we should.'

'That character's got some funny notions,' said the engineer. 'He asked me if I could fix him up some heavy duty lasers to use in his defences. Can you beat that?'

'Can you do it?'

'Not without a lot of time and a lot of machine work,' said Longridge. 'We've got some lasers, sure, but they're working tools. Cutter and drills and stuff like that. Some of them could be used as weapons if they had to be. Hell, anything could if it comes to that. Webb seems to think that I can rig him up a sort of heat ray. Just aim, press, and bingo ! No more opposition.'

'He's got a point,' said Easton thoughtfully. 'Maybe we should have thought of it before.'

'Maybe,' admitted Longridge. 'But we had a few other things to think of too. Remember?'

Too many other things, thought Easton.

A damn sight too many. But we could have made a mistake, he told himself. We could have missed some good ideas by trying to do everything at once. By being too busy to ask or listen. But we had no choice, he thought. We had to dive in at the deep end. 'How is the honeycomb holding out?'

Longridge shrugged. 'It isn't,' he said flatly. 'The liquid helium has all evaporated. I've managed to store it and we can liquefy it again if we have to but it'll be a long job. This climate's too hot and too damp,' he said. 'There's too much conducted heat. Trying to keep the helium circulating in the honeycomb would have been a full-time job.'

'All right,' said Easton. 'It doesn't matter.' They had woken all the living, human cargo. The rest hadn't come aboard. The cows and horses, pigs and sheep, dogs, cats, and chickens. They had all been left behind. 'You'd better get going,' he said. 'Giving Fred a hand?'

'Of course,' Longridge grinned. 'People who work in cookhouses never go hungry,' he said meaningfully. 'And those who work in bars don't go thirsty. I figure to work in both.'

★   ★   ★

Easton entered the ship. The upper levels were kept tightly sealed and it took time for him to operate the locks and climb up to the computer room. Adrienne was at her usual station. She looked up as he entered the compartment and then became furiously busy. He sat and watched her.

'You wanted something?' She spoke when the silence was beginning to become embarrassing. Her neck, he saw, was a little flushed, her breathing a little fast.

'I came to remind you that Doris was having her party tonight,' he said. 'Her birthday party. Are you going?'

'I've got a headache.'

'Real or diplomatic?' He waited for an answer. 'Look,' he said finally. 'If you're sick report to the doctors. If you're not how about showing a little common politeness? You know how Doris feels about these things. She's sentimental.'

The girl didn't answer.

'She likes you, Adrienne.'

'So?'

'So why must you be such a bitch?' He resisted the desire to reach out, grip her slim shoulders and shake her until she revealed some kind of emotion. Anger, even, that would be better than the distant hostility which seemed to envelop her like a second skin. 'It wouldn't take much to drop over,' he said reasonably. 'Have a drink or two and wish her a happy birthday. I know she'd appreciate it.'

'I don't really care what Doris appreciates,' said Adrienne flatly. She turned on her chair, facing him, her eyes distant. 'Did you come here just to tell me that or was it for some other reason?'

'I'm sending Rodgers out soon,' he said coldly. 'I want you to plot a course, decide on the most favourable areas for exploration, check on the weather. I also want you to monitor his fuel consumption and allow a decent safety margin. You can trim the permitted mileage you give him for operational purposes. I want him to get back.'

'What do you want him to do?'

'Fly north,' said Easton. 'Way north. I want to find out what is happening up there. Williams can go with him. I want to settle the question of the stability of this area as soon as possible.'

'Anything else?'

Yes, he thought, a lot of things. I'd like you to thaw out and rejoin the human race. To forget what happened during the journey or, if you can't forget, try and understand. Love isn't and can never be the most important thing in a man's life. Not when he has a ship to worry about, a crew to take care of, a civilization to transplant. Not when he's tired and beginning to doubt himself. 'Nothing specific,' he said. 'Just the usual.'

'I understand,' said Adrienne. 'He's to keep a sharp lookout for signs of intelligent life.' Her eyes softened a little as she looked at the captain. 'It's on your mind, isn't it? It's been on your mind ever since we landed. But he can't be here,' she said. 'Wherever Holmson crashed it can't be here. He saw something. We didn't. What he saw could be on the other side of the planet.'

'I know,' said Easton.

'There must be a lot of rivers which loop. A lot of mountains showing smoke.'

'I know,' said Easton again. 'But that isn't the point. Something is down here. Holmson saw them and they must exist. We just can't pretend they don't.'

'He could have been excited,' she suggested. 'Upset. Not seeing things too clearly. It was just before he crashed, remember. He could have been confused.'

'You're wrong,' said Easton tiredly. 'You're forgetting the exact sequence of events. I haven't. I've listened to that tape until I hear it in my sleep. Holmson was in full control and nothing was wrong. He became excited only after he saw what was down here. He was startled, incredulous, but he wasn't confused. Then we jerked into M-space. Holmson could have crashed or he could have been shot down. He could have died or he could still be alive. All we know for sure is that he didn't answer the radio.'

'He could be a prisoner,' she said thoughtfully. 'Or even free but hopelessly lost somewhere.'

'Yes,' said Easton.

'And there's nothing we can do about it,' she said. 'Not a damn thing.'

'No,' he said. 'There isn't. We haven't enough fuel for the helicopter to make a really good search. We can't use the auxiliary because it travels too fast and because we don't want whoever is down here to come looking for us. I'm not so worried about us finding them,' he explained, 'as in them finding us. We'd be at too great a disadvantage.'

'War,' she said. 'You're thinking of war.'

'I'm thinking of survival,' he corrected. 'Our survival.'

'There's a difference?'

'A hell of a difference. I want us to stay alive. If I have to kill in order for us to do that, then I'll kill.' He rose to his feet. 'It's the old law of the jungle,' he said flatly. 'It's carried us up from the caves to the stars. Two million years have shown that it works. That's good enough for me.'

Alone she sat and stared at the

mechanical face of the computer. It stared back with its dials and meters, lights and tell-tales. By them she could read Easton's progress through the ship as he moved away from her, down the stairs, through the locks, on to the outside. Walking away from me, she thought. Leaving me behind.

She blinked at the sharp burning of her eyes.

He could have asked, she thought. I could have got up and got ready and gone with him to the party. We could have had some drinks and talked and laughed a little, and maybe things would have been as they used to be. We could have become close and, maybe, he would have kissed me and looked on me as a woman instead of a useful member of his damned crew. Why the hell didn't he ask?

Because he knew, she told herself. He knew that you wouldn't have gone with him, and you'd have said something smart and hurtful, getting your revenge like some silly child. And he doesn't want to be hurt. He doesn't want to give you the opportunity of making him feel small.

Or perhaps, she thought, he just doesn't care.

This time she didn't fight her tears.

★ ★ ★

'Listen to them.' Roy Seegan leaned against the jamb of the open door of the dormitory hut. 'They must be having a ball,' he said enviously. 'Quite a ball.'

'Sure.' Charles Pierce joined him and stood looking out into the night. It was dark aside from the dim glow of the guard posts, the scattered illumination of the beacons, the light spilling from the windows and doors of the various huts. Across the landing field Trebor's workroom was a halo of illumination. Music came from behind the high screens he'd erected around the area. Music and the sound of laughter.

'That must be some party.' Seegan sucked in his breath. 'Drink and music,' he said. 'Girls and a good time.'

'For them,' said Pierce. 'Not for us.'

'Webb's joined them.'

'Sure, Webb has, but not us.' Pierce

twisted the knife. 'They don't want us,' he said. 'They've got no time for you and me. We don't belong. We can guard their damn camp and do all the hard work but when it comes to the bit of relaxation we're at the end of the line.'

'That isn't fair,' said a voice from behind. Jim Radford looked towards the lights and music. 'It's a private party,' he said. 'They asked the people they wanted. They couldn't invite everyone.'

Pierce made a sound of contempt.

'It's true,' insisted Radford. 'Webb explained it to me. He's going to see if he can get a jug sent down to us. So we can join in the toast,' he explained. 'Drink to Doris's health.'

'Charity,' said Pierce. 'Goddam charity. They can stuff their damn jug.'

'That's right,' echoed Seegan.

Radford shrugged. 'I'm just telling you what Webb told me,' he said. 'I don't know what you're getting all steamed up about. A few people get together for a few drinks. Does that give us the right to demand that we should be allowed to join in?'

'It's our stuff they're using,' said Pierce spitefully. 'Our food, our drink, our goddam protection. If Trebor had to sweat it out in the guard lines he wouldn't have had time to make his brew. But what do you expect?' he demanded. 'We're scum and they're letting us know it. Good enough to stand guard and get killed by the hoppers but not good enough to be invited in for a drink. A lousy drink,' he said. 'A single lousy drink. They could have given us that.'

'Not them,' said Seegan. His big hands clenched as he stared towards the party. 'Just like back home,' he said. 'We do all the work and they get all the gravy.'

'What else did you expect?' said Pierce. 'We're expendable. They can do without us.' He turned, looked at Radford. 'How do you feel about it?'

Radford didn't answer.

'Look,' said Pierce. 'You were snatched. You've been made to work without pay. You stand a good chance of getting yourself killed. Did you have any money back home?'

'A few dollars,' admitted Radford. 'Not much.'

'None of us had much,' said Pierce, 'but it was all we had. I had a mother,' he lied. 'She depended on me. I used to send her cash so that she could keep going. What's going to happen to her now?'

'We've been robbed,' said Seegan. 'They've treated us like dirt.'

'They've broken the law,' said Pierce. 'We're entitled to do anything we can. If we kill them it wouldn't be murder.' He paused then, 'You want to be a slave all your life?'

'No, but — '

'Then what are you going to do about it?'

'Easton explained all that,' said Radford. He had the feeling that he was being swept along by a torrent. 'So did Webb. We all have to work together so that we can get settled. Then, when things are established, we can take our place. Farm our own land,' he said. 'Run our own businesses. Be equal. Anyway,' he added, 'Easton said that we'd all be dead by now if he hadn't taken us along.'

'You believe that?'

Radford hesitated.

'He robs you blind, sets you to work without pay in this stinking hole and then he tells you that he's done you a favour.' Pierce shook his head. 'Man,' he said, 'how dumb can you get? If you swallow that you're a first-class dope.'

'Jim's no dope,' said Seegan. 'I'll talk to him, Charlie. You just leave this to me. I'll talk to him good.'

Pierce nodded and stepped outside the hut, melting into the shadows as he leaned back against the wall. Across the landing field the lights of the party made a splotch of warmth and brilliance. The music and laughter seemed very loud.

Go on, he thought sourly. Laugh, drink, enjoy yourselves. It'll be my turn soon. And it would have to be soon. You can't trust anyone, he told himself. There was always someone who would spill the beans. I've got to move before they get the chance, he thought. I've got to hit hard and fast and without warning.

He looked around as Seegan came from the hut. 'Here,' he called. 'I'm over here.' The big man was alone. 'Radford?'

'I hit him,' said Seegan. He rubbed his fist. 'He wouldn't see things our way. I was scared that he'd go running to Webb.' He hesitated. 'I hit him damn hard,' he confessed. 'I think he's dead.'

'It doesn't matter.'

'I didn't mean to kill him. I was scared and hit harder than I thought.'

'It doesn't matter,' said Pierce again. He stood, thinking. 'Put him in his bunk,' he decided. 'He won't be missed until dawn when we go on duty. That's when we hit.' He looked at the other man, enjoying his moment. 'We may never get a better chance,' he explained. 'They're all together at the party, drinking, having themselves a ball, getting half-stoned. They'll be tired if nothing else. We'll hit when we go down to relieve the guard.'

'Take over the ship?'

'That's right.'

Seegan frowned. 'Can we?' he demanded. 'I mean, if we take it what can we do with it?'

'Anything we damn well like,' said Pierce. 'I've been finding out a few things,' he added. 'The ship has a tin pilot. You tell it what to do and it does it. We don't need anyone to run the ship, a ten-year-old kid could do it. All we have to do is to get inside, seal it up and we'll be sitting pretty. Easton does as we want or it's too bad for Easton.'

'He'll take us back home?'

'If we want to go,' said Pierce. 'But maybe we won't want that. Not right away.'

'You're wrong,' said Seegan. 'When we take over the ship we go home. Make no mistake about that.'

'All right,' said Pierce.

'What about Easton?'

'He stays behind. Him and any of the others who want to stay. They can have it,' said Pierce. 'They can have the whole damn stinking planet all to themselves.'

★ ★ ★

Longridge was drunk. He stood at the entrance to the enclosure and sang a song he had learned when at college — the unexpurgated version. The bikini-clad blonde at his side didn't seem to mind. When he had finished she poured him another drink from the jug standing at her feet.

'Hey there!' Longridge swayed as he waved at the captain. 'You're missing all the fun. Meet Julie.'

'Hello, Julie,' said Easton.

'Hello, captain.' The girl was almost as far gone as the engineer. She offered Easton her glass. 'Have a drink.'

'No, thanks. I promised to have the first one with Doris,' he said hastily. 'You wouldn't want me to break a promise would you?'

'No,' she said.

'The ol' captain never broke a promise in his life,' said Longridge. 'That's one thing I like about the captain. He never breaks a promise.'

'He's a good guy,' said the girl.

'Have fun,' said Easton. He moved away to where a table had been set up before Trebor's workroom. Doris frowned as he approached.

'You're late,' she accused.

'I know. I had work to do,' he

explained. 'I took a walk around the perimeter.' He turned, looking at the crowd.

'She isn't here,' said Doris. 'Adrienne, I mean. That's who you were looking for, wasn't it?'

He nodded.

'Never mind,' she said. 'Have a drink of this special blend.'

The liquid was amber with an unmistakable odour. He sipped, rolled it around his tongue, finally swallowed. Warmth climbed from his stomach. 'Not bad,' he said to Doris. 'Not bad at all.'

'I'm glad you like it,' she said, smiling. 'Fred worked hard on that. He worked hard on the rest of the stuff too, the wine, beer, and canapes, but he really took trouble over the whisky.'

'It was worth it.' Easton took another sip then raised his glass. 'To you,' he said. 'Many happy returns of the day. At least a hundred of them.'

'Thank you.' She waited until he had emptied his glass. 'Like another?'

'I'd better,' said Easton. 'While it lasts.' And that, he thought looking at the crowd, wouldn't be long.

The party was going with a swing. Taped music jarred the air with cacophonous rhythm, fighting a losing battle with the hum of conversation, laughter, impromptu song. Alcohol, he thought. The universal solvent. One thing which could turn enemies into friends, despair into a joke, make tomorrow seem worth living for. He took a sip of his refilled glass. After long abstinence the stuff seemed to have the kick of a mule. I'd better go easy, he told himself. The captain, at least, should remain sober.

'Like something to eat?' Trebor, his face flushed and happy, shoved his way towards the captain. He carried a big tray loaded with delicacies. 'Go on,' he urged. 'Try some.'

Easton picked a thing which looked like a strawberry. It tasted like one, too. He followed it with a date, a slice of apple, a crystallized pear.

'Yeast,' said Trebor. 'What the hell would we do without it? The booze, the food, all yeast. Bred, twisted, shaped, and flavoured to taste. The whole damn shooting match is nothing but yeast.'

Trebor had obviously been sampling his products with a little too much enthusiasm. Well, thought Easton, so what? The man had worked hard for his pleasure. 'You've done well,' he said. 'Damn well.'

'Me and the yeast,' corrected Trebor.

'Sure,' said Easton. 'You and the yeast.'

He moved through the crowd, knowing better than to look but looking just the same. Adrienne wasn't at the party. She meant it, he thought. The damn stubborn little bitch! He took another swallow of his drink. It burned his mouth, throat and stomach, adding to the heat of the night, the almost suffocating humidity aggravated by the complete absence of any kind of breeze.

He felt irritable, out of sympathy with those around him. Their laughter jarred as did the music. It's been too long, he thought. I've forgotten how to relax. That's the thing about worry, he told himself. You live with it so long that it becomes a part of you and then, when there's nothing to worry about, you worry because of that. But, on Eden, there was always something to worry about.

He paused beside two men who were examining something. Meldew looked up and nodded. 'Did you see this?' he asked. He was holding a woman's handbag of some unfamiliar material. 'Hopper hide,' he explained. 'Webb gave a skin to a couple of his boys and they've been working on it. It's their present to Doris.'

'I helped them tan it,' said the other man. His name was Greene and he'd once worked in a leather shop. 'It wasn't easy,' he added. 'The stuff's as tough as steel.'

'Very nice.' Easton examined the material. It had a hard, soapy feel and was too inflexible to make a good leather for the purpose, but he could appreciate the thought behind the gift. 'It should make good shoes,' he said.

Greene nodded. 'Maybe I'll try it,' he said. 'When I get a chance to set up a factory.'

'You will,' said Easton. He looked around. 'Have you seen Webb?'

'He was here a moment ago,' said

Meldew. 'I guess that he stepped outside.'

The blond was standing about fifteen yards from the enclosure, his thumbs in their usual position, the web between thumb and first finger pressing down on his belt. He was looking towards the north. Far distant, almost at the edge of vision, lightning flickered in transient brightness over the mountains.

'Heat lightning,' said Easton. 'Maybe we'll have a storm.'

'Maybe.' Webb pursed his lips. 'We could do with it,' he said. 'This damn humidity's getting past a joke. A storm could clear the air.' His eyes dropped to the captain's waist. 'Is that thing loaded and ready to go?'

'My pistol? Yes.'

'Let me see it.'

Easton passed over the gun. It was a 7.65mm thirty shot automatic. Webb removed the magazine, jerked the slide and deftly caught the cartridge as it spun in the air. He replaced it in the magazine and rammed it home. He operated the slide and handed back the pistol. 'No,' he said as Easton began to ease forward the hammer. 'Don't do that.'

'You want me to leave it fully cocked and ready to fire?'

'That's right,' said Webb. 'You've got a butt safety on that model,' he explained. 'You won't have an accident. But there might not be time for you to cock the gun or to release the usual safety catch. You might forget or fumble. And,' he added, 'that could be fatal.'

'You expect trouble?'

'Yes,' said Webb. 'I've been expecting it for days. It's a feeling I've got. I — ' He broke off, cursing, as something climbed into the sky at the edge of the settlement. It exploded with a vivid gush of crimson.

10

'Red alarm,' said Webb. His face in the dying light of the flare looked strained and tense, a Viking glaring into the heart of hell. Thrusting his fingers into his mouth he blew three shrill blasts. Turning he ran towards the party and yelled into the enclosure. 'Cut the music! Cut it!'

Doris turned off the player. In the following silence they could hear the sound from the perimeter, the sharp, spiteful sound of firing rifles. Webb repeated his signal.

'Washa marrer?' Longridge came staggering from the enclosure. 'Wash up?'

'Get back in there!' Webb's eyes searched the crowd. 'Meldew! You're sober. Get the drunks into the hut and keep them there. The women too. Send as many men as can stand and use a gun to action stations. Move!' He glared into the darkness. 'Where the hell are the lights?' he demanded. 'Where's that damn truck?'

He whistled again. Lights blazed around the perimeter as someone switched on the giant floods. The firing increased. Someone screamed, the sound thin and unreal in the distance. An electric truck came whining towards the enclosure. The open back was filled with armed men, most of them barely awake. It braked. Webb and Easton climbed aboard.

'Guard post seven,' said the driver as he spun the wheel. He swore as other flares climbed into the sky. 'Six and two! Hell, this looks like a big one!'

Easton made no comment. He clung to the side of the truck as the driver fed power to the motors, sending the vehicle whining towards the edge of the settlement. The direct route lay through a patch of growing wheat. He took the direct route.

'Stop behind the posts,' ordered Webb. 'Then go and get some more men.' He looked at Easton. 'You shouldn't be here,' he said. 'This is my job.'

'I'm staying.'

'Yes,' said Webb. 'I guess you are.'

The truck slid to a halt. The men riding

in the back jumped down and deployed to either side. The firing increased, rising to a crescendo, then became sporadic, finally dying to be taken up further down the line. Webb drew his pistol and ran forward. Easton almost trod on his heels.

The guard post was a hole dug in the ground protected by a breastwork and roof of thick logs. A floodlight was mounted on the roof with others to either side. The gaps between the lights were too great to give absolute coverage. In the glare Easton could see the main line of defence, a series of rifle pits sunk into the dirt. Before and around them slumped a litter of dead hoppers. A few had managed to jump the pits to be brought down by the guard post. Behind the post sprawled the defenceless settlement.

'How bad?' Webb snapped at the post commander, a young man with a shock of black hair.

'Pretty bad while it lasted,' said the commander. He glowered at a dead hopper lying arm's length from the defensive wall. 'They came at us in a sudden wave. I lost a couple of men before we could get into action, a few more before we could stop the rush.'

'Bad enough,' said Webb grimly. He yelled to the men he had brought with him. 'Half of you go and collect any wounded. The rest of you cover them.' He looked at Easton. 'It's a waste of time,' he admitted. 'Any wounded are as good as dead from that damned poison. But we've got to go through the motions for the sake of morale.'

A telephone buzzed within the guard post. The young commander lifted the receiver, listened, answered, replaced the handset. 'Guard post two,' he commented. 'They've beaten off the attack and want to know if we need any help.' He looked outside. 'We don't,' he said. 'I guess we've wiped out this bunch all along the line.'

Webb nodded, listening to the firing. Aside from a few scattered shots it had completely died away. After a moment even the few shots fell into silence. From somewhere came the whimper of a wounded man. A gun fired. The whimper ceased.

'They're learning,' said the post commander grimly. 'The hoppers aim for the guts. A disembowelled man can linger for quite a while sometimes. Most of them choose not to do it.'

'They're smart,' said Webb. He frowned at the dead hopper lying before the guard post. He jumped the barrier and went to it. He kicked it, examined the feet, kicked it again.

'Something wrong?' Easton joined the blond man.

'I'm not sure,' said Webb slowly. 'I've studied the hoppers and something doesn't fit. This one has been travelling fast and far, the feet tell you that. Yet its stomach is full. When they eat they sleep. This one didn't. Why?'

'Are they all like that?'

'Let's find out,' said Webb. He stopped after they'd examined a dozen. 'They're all the same. Enough so as to make no real difference.' He stared thoughtfully towards the north. 'They always come from up there,' he said. 'From the high and rocky ground.'

'So?'

'The hoppers we've just killed had travelled a long way. By rights they shouldn't have tried to rush us. They weren't hungry and it's usually hunger that drives them towards the settlement. The overspill from the local population explosion,' he explained. 'I've been talking to Barman and Meldew about it. They both agree.'

'You're trying to say something,' said Easton. 'What is it?'

'I'm thinking of a forest fire,' said Webb. 'You know how it is. A fire gets started and every living thing runs from the flames. Fear is contagious. Animals who haven't even seen the fire or smelt the smoke join in the rush. It turns into a stampede and only stops when they hit a natural barrier or drop from exhaustion.' He paused. 'I'm wondering just how many hoppers are up there in the north,' he said. 'And how far they have to come.'

'Pressure,' said Easton. He thought of the smoke they had seen, the lightning. 'You think that this was the first wave? That more is to come?'

'I could be wrong,' said Webb.

'Yes,' said Easton. 'I hope to God that you are.'

★ ★ ★

'Now,' said Pierce. He reared up and squinted over the edge of the rifle pit. A hopper looked back at him, the ruby eyes dulled by death. Behind the pit a floodlight mounted on the roof of guard post five threw a harsh glare over the terrain. Shadows looked like black, paper cut-outs. The air reeked with the stink of cordite though the firing had ceased.

'How can we?' Seegan crouched in the pit. His face was white, strained. Death had twice come very close. 'They'll see us,' he pointed out. 'If we try to leave now they'll spot us for sure.'

'Not if we shoot out the light.'

'You're crazy,' said Seegan. 'Crazy!'

No, thought Pierce, I'm not crazy, just in one hell of a situation. He clamped his hands around the stock of his rifle, raging in frustrated anger. I had it planned, he told himself. I had it all worked out down to the last detail. Wait until dawn when everyone's tired and things are blurred by the dawn mist. Hit fast and hard. Before anyone would know it I'd be in full control. Damn the hoppers! he raged. Why the hell did they have to attack now?

He forced himself to be calm.

Think, he told himself. Use your brains. So the original plan is a bust, so what? The ship is still there, isn't it? I can still take over control. The details have altered, that's all. He glowered at the dead hopper, remembering how he had jerked from sleep to the yell of shouted orders, the hurry and bustle, the men clustering around leaving no chance to slip away. The only good thing was that the action had been so frenzied no one had noticed Radford's absence. But they will, he told himself. They will.

'Look,' he said to Seegan. 'We've got no choice. If we don't act now we'll never get another chance.'

'They'll shoot us,' said Seegan. 'They'll spot us and gun us down.' He reared up and looked towards the light. 'They're in there,' he said. 'In the guard post. Watching. If you try to shoot out the light they'll see you. If we try to leave the same. Damn it,' he said. 'We're stuck in this goddamned pit like flies on treacle. We can't move.'

'We'd better,' said Pierce. 'Or rather you had.'

'Why me?'

'You killed Radford.'

'You — '

'Sure,' said Pierce. 'I heard about it. I agreed with it. But you did it. Don't forget that.'

Seegan glowered from the side of the pit.

'I'm with you,' said Pierce hastily. 'I'm not letting you down. We made a deal, remember? We're in this together. But they're going to find Radford and when they do they'll ask questions. They'll shoot you,' he said. 'They may even hang you.'

'No!' Seegan shook his head. 'They can't do that. It was an accident.'

'Sure,' said Pierce. 'You know it and I know it but will the others believe it? You're a big man,' he pointed out. 'Strong. Radford wasn't. They'll call it murder.'

'Help me,' said Seegan. 'You're smart, Charlie. You've got to help me.'

'Listen.' Pierce lifted his rifle. 'When I fire you give a yell. Yell as if you'd been shot.'

'And?'

'Leave the rest to me. Ready?' He aimed the rifle at the ground. 'Now!'

He fired. Seegan yelled. A voice called from the guard post. 'What goes on down there?'

'Seegan's hurt,' called back Pierce. 'His gun went off and got him in the leg. He's bleeding bad.' He threw his rifle over the edge of the pit, climbed out, dragged Seegan after him. 'Groan,' he whispered. 'Hang on me as if you can't stand. Limp on the right leg. The right leg, dammit!'

He stooped, picked up his rifle and, with Seegan hanging around his neck, moved slowly towards the rear. The voice called to him as he approached the guard post. 'You'd better take him straight to the doctors. Need any help?'

'No, thanks,' said Pierce. 'I can manage.'

'Put a tourniquet on him,' advised the

voice. 'You don't want him to bleed to death.'

'I'll do that,' said Pierce. He breathed a sigh of relief as they moved past the edge of brightness into the comparative darkness beyond. 'Done it,' he whispered. 'The sucker fell for it.'

'We take over the ship now, Charlie?'

'Sure,' said Pierce. 'We take over the ship.'

Barman aimed the hypogun, triggered the charge, watched as the rat went limp. He thrust a gloved hand into the cage and removed the body. The young were already dead. 'Experiment number twenty-three,' he said emotionlessly. 'Negative.'

Celia made a note on her pad then looked at the biomech. 'What now?'

'Nothing.' He looked at the interior of the hut, the glistening instruments and apparatus. 'Nothing more here, anyway. This place is contaminated. I don't know what I'm doing anymore. From now on we'll have to work in the ship.' He threw the dead rat into a disposal container.

'Do you think you'll ever be able to solve the problem?'

He shrugged. 'I don't know. Maybe, given enough time and a hell of a lot of luck. But I wouldn't take bets on it.'

He moved to the open door and stood looking outside. The thin sound of firing had ceased and, he thought, I should be busy soon with the injured. But he knew better. The hoppers were either killed or they killed in turn. There would be no wounded.

He turned a little and looked towards Trebor's hut. A hell of a way to end a party, he thought. Just when things were beginning to go with a real swing. He licked his lips, remembering the taste of the whisky, wishing he had a bottle so as to be able to take a drink now. A lot of drinks. I could use them, he told himself. Sometimes you can see things more clearly through the bottom of a bottle. At least, he thought, I might as well be drinking as working at a dead end, experimenting and clearing up just for the sake of something to do.

'Do you remember what one of Webb's boys said?' he asked over his shoulder. 'At the party I mean. When we were looking at that handbag they made for Doris.'

'No,' she lied. 'I don't remember.'

'He said that it was lucky I hadn't made it.' Barman felt the muscles knot along the line of his jaw. 'He said that, if I had, it would have probably been made of human skin.'

'He was joking,' she said.

'A hell of a joke. You know,' he said. 'That man really hated me.'

'He's a little afraid of you,' she said. 'It isn't the same thing.'

'Maybe not.' Barman leaned against the jamb, his eyes drifting over the settlement. An arc of light blazed along the perimeter. Other lights shone from huts and sheds. The ship was bathed in it. The sky held the oddly liquid translucence of imminent dawn. Between him and the ship the growing corn made a tasselled carpet of delicate tracery, grey in the subdued light. 'We did it all wrong,' he said quietly, speaking almost to himself. 'We should have taken our time, run tests, made certain. Now it's too late for that.'

He felt the woman join him.

'We put all our eggs into one basket,' he

said. 'Or Easton did. He took a gamble and he's lost.'

She said nothing, listening.

'I had plans,' he said. 'Big plans. You may have guessed them. This was to be a new beginning. This was to be the end of hampering superstition and false values. For once science was to get the chance to show what it could do. Here, on a new world, with the knowledge we have, we could have built utopia.'

'Whose utopia?' she asked quietly. 'Yours?'

'Ours. All of us.'

'No,' she said. 'No matter how it would have turned out it could never have been that. No utopia ever can. Everyone has their own idea of perfection and no one can ever fully realize it. Life is a continuous compromise. Always we have to give a little. Always we have to settle for only a part of what we really want. That's life, Jud. Real life. Not the isolated dreams of an idealist.'

'You think so?'

'I know so,' she said. 'Believe me, Jud, I know.'

'Yes,' he said. 'I guess that you do.' He turned and faced her. 'I've got a lot to learn,' he admitted. 'Will you teach me?'

'As your colleague, Jud?'

'No,' he said. 'As my wife.'

★ ★ ★

Easton heard the news as he came from the perimeter in the grey light of early dawn. Behind him, beyond the rifle pits, between them and the forest, great fires burned as they disposed of the litter of dead hoppers. He blinked reddened eyes, staring at Webb. 'The ship?' he said. 'Are you serious?'

'Listen,' said Webb patiently. He could see that the captain hadn't fully grasped what he had to say. 'We've lost control of the ship,' he repeated. 'A couple of men sneaked in during or after the attack. Pierce and Seegan,' he said. 'You wouldn't know them. A couple of men you had snatched from the project. Bums,' he added. 'No-goods. Born trouble-makers.'

'How did it happen?'

'I don't know for sure,' admitted Webb. 'My guess is that they simply walked in and had the doors sealed after them. They killed a guard doing it,' he said grimly. 'The only one stationed at the vessel. They shot him and stole his pistol. They must have tricked the pilot into sealing the ship.'

'The pilot,' said Easton. 'Or Adrienne.'

'That's right,' said Webb. He hadn't mentioned the girl. The captain had enough trouble as it was. 'I tried to get in,' he continued. 'I couldn't. I phoned and Pierce answered. The cocky sonofabitch sounded quite pleased with himself.'

'What does he want?' asked Easton.

'He wants to take over,' said Webb.

'Everything?'

'The works. He told me to pass the word. He'll take anyone who wants to go back home with him. Aside from you,' he added. 'And me. He won't take us at any price.' Webb stared up at the soaring hulk of the ship. 'He said one more thing. The girl, Adrienne. He's got her as a hostage. We try anything and he blows her head off.'

'He would,' said Easton. 'Did he give a time limit?'

'One day,' said Webb. 'One lousy day.'

'We've got to get them out,' decided Easton.

It was a problem. The ship was sealed, airtight, closed to entry. To use explosives was both to damage the hull and to scare those inside to precipitate action. The venturis were blocked by the radioactive danger of the reactors. The pilot would warn against any attempt to burn or force a way through the structure. The pilot?

'Adrienne's no fool,' said Easton thoughtfully. 'And she's got guts. She wouldn't have told them any more than she had to. Those characters might think they've got control of the ship but my guess is they haven't. Not full control anyway. Get Rodgers.'

Webb relayed the command.

'Can you lift me to the top of the ship?' asked Easton when the pilot arrived. 'I want to be suspended under your bird and held steady over the exact summit.'

'I can lift you, sure,' said the pilot. 'About the rest I don't know. There's a rising wind along the hull of the ship. Just what did you have in mind?' He pursed his lips in a soundless whistle as Easton told him. 'It's crazy,' he said. 'Crazy.'

'Can you do it?'

'It's your neck,' said Rodgers. 'If you're willing to take a chance then so am I.'

An hour later the helicopter took off, Easton crouched in the cabin beside the open door. Rodgers had decided that it would be better that way. He looked at the captain as they rose, climbing into the sky while the settlement shrank beneath, wheeling so as to ride above the pointed nose of the ship. 'All right,' he said. 'Let yourself down.'

Easton nodded and stepped through the open door. Rope held him to the seat structure, the loop of the slack hanging beneath the machine. Other rope hung in a long loop from his waist, held by a system of eyes and a complicated pulley. He checked his equipment and stepped into thin air. The rope jerked at his shoulders. Slowly he let it slide through his fingers until he hung suspended at the end, ten yards below the chopper.

There could be no further instructions. Rodgers would do the best he could and that was all. The rest depended on luck, memory, the stretching power of the rope and sheer nerve. The helicopter swayed a little and Easton began to pendulum beneath the cabin. He swore, holding the long loop of rope in his hands, spreading it wide for the cast. The nose of the ship swung towards him and he tossed the rope.

He missed.

He tried again, trying to ignore the ache in his arms, the savage jerking of his belt, the giddy manoeuvrings of the machine, the blast of air from the rotors. He missed again, a third time. Desperately he widened the loop still more and, as Rodgers swung him towards the target, flung the rope over the nose. It hit, hesitated, then the loop slipped down, sticking as the nose widened to fill the loop. Easton clawed a knife from his belt, lifted his arm, slashed at the rope holding him to the helicopter. The strands frayed, parted, and he fell like a stone.

Fell to slam against the hull of the ship

as the loop checked his fall.

The knife slipped from his fingers. He felt dazed, bruised, semi-conscious. Dimly he saw the metal before his face, heard the dying roar of the helicopter as it swung away. Hanging like a fly against an icicle he reviewed his position.

He hung a few yards from the apex of the ship, the rope loop circling the hull with himself hanging from it. He tugged at the pulley and managed to feed out more rope. The loop widened and he dropped lower. He planted his feet against the hull and reared back, searching for a way in. He circled the hull twice before he found it, the thin crack of the upper entry port. It was below and to one side. He fed out more rope, leaning back so as to force it through the pulley. His feet slipped and he slammed hard against the hull, not so hard as the first time but hard enough to send pain through his chest and put the taste of blood in his mouth.

He kicked and swung out and to one side. He kicked again and the port was before him. All he had to do was to open it. It would, he thought, take him about thirty minutes with luck, a couple of hours if at all without. To help him he had the laser from the repair shop. He blinked as the beam began to sear the metal.

*   *   *

Pierce sat in the control chair, his legs thrust out before him, his head leaning comfortably against the padding of the seat. He was looking at one of the screens which showed activity to one side of the settlement. Men and women milled around like a nest of disturbed ants. He chuckled as he saw them. 'They're worried,' he said. 'They know we've got the upper hand. They're scared yellow in case we leave them to rot.'

'Maybe we should at that,' suggested Seegan. He sat in one of the other chairs, the rifle leaning against the panel. 'We've got all we want,' he pointed out. 'The ship, food, someone to cheer us up when we're lonely.'

Adrienne sat silently at her panel. She didn't look at either of the men.

'She's a snotty little bitch,' said Pierce blandly. 'Teaching her a lesson would be a pleasure.'

He relaxed, smiling, one hand falling to the butt of the pistol tucked into his belt. It had been easy, he thought. So damned easy. One guard, one shot and the ship was theirs. The girl too, he told himself, though she had been a bonus. A starchy bitch who needed warming up but he didn't think he'd take the trouble to do it. There were others who would be grateful for the chance to ride home. Plenty of others.

'We'll take the doctor,' said Seegan dreamily. 'The female one. Then the chemist, Doris, and we might as well take her old man. Who else?'

'Everyone else,' said Pierce. 'All but that cowson Webb and the captain. 'We'll take them all — just as long as they know who is the boss. But we don't have to,' he said speaking to the girl. 'We can take off now if I feel like it. Isn't that right?'

He waited for an answer. When none came he reached out and dug his fingers in her short, red hair. 'Listen,' he said, and twisted his grip. 'When I talk you listen. When I want an answer you give me one. Understand?'

'Yes,' she said.

'That's better.' He twisted a little harder. 'The ship is all ready to go, isn't it?'

'Yes.'

'The tanks loaded and everything?' His hand twisted even harder. 'Answer,' he said. 'Answer before I tear your damn scalp off.'

'The ship is ready to go.'

'That's better.' He released his grip. 'In a little while we'll have a talk,' he promised. 'A good long talk.'

In a little while you'll be dead, she thought savagely. I'll kill you if I have to go the same way myself. You deserve it, she told herself. You acted the fool and let these swine into the sealed area. You believed them and closed the hull. You've asked for everything you've got. She looked at the control panels. Lights relayed their message, telling of the condition of the vessel. She kept her face expressionless.

'I want to talk to the tin-head which runs this thing,' said Pierce. 'The pilot. How do I do it?'

'You can't.'

'Try again, baby.' He reached for her hair. 'Try real hard.'

'It's conditioned to operate only to certain voices,' she said. 'A sonic barrier against unauthorized use. If you speak to it it won't answer.'

'Will it answer you?'

'No,' she lied. 'Only the captain and the engineer.'

'That doesn't make sense,' said Pierce thoughtfully. 'The ship left with only a small crew. You could have got into trouble at any time. What would have happened if the captain and Longridge had fallen sick at the same time? Or died?' He shook his head. 'You're lying,' he said. 'You keep lying. Maybe I should teach you a lesson you'll never forget.'

'Teach me,' suggested Easton softly. He stepped through the open door of the control room and saw the white blur of startled faces. He fired as Seegan made a grab at the rifle, aiming low as Webb had instructed, the pistol tight in his hand. He fired again as the man spun, a third time as he fell to the floor.

'Damn you!' Pierce snatched at his gun, his face contorted with rage and fear. 'Damn you!'

He doubled as a bullet smashed into his stomach. He tried to straighten, to lift his pistol, then slumped as three more bullets seared into his body.

'David!' Adrienne stood, pale with shock and relief. 'David!'

'It's all right,' he said. 'I came through the upper port. I guessed they would be watching the lower entries but I took a chance that they wouldn't know about the tell-tales.'

'I hadn't told them,' she admitted. 'But I didn't know that you were coming. We've been in here all the time,' she explained. 'I hadn't notified the pilot to activate the repeaters so I didn't know what was going on. I — ' She broke off, blinking back her tears, the hard façade of her defence crumbling. 'David. I've been such a fool!'

'We've both been fools,' he said. 'And

I've been the bigger.'

He felt her against him, the warm softness of her body, the touch of her lips on his blistering face. He breathed the scent of her hair. After a long while she stepped back, her eyes shining. 'David, I love you,' she said. 'And I know that you love me. From now on everything's going to be wonderful.'

She made it sound so beautifully simple.

11

The attack came at noon, hitting just after the helicopter had buzzed to the north, boiling from the woods in the mid-day heat. A dirty green tide of bouncing death as the hoppers lunged from cover towards the settlement. Rifle fire crackled as the defenders shot them down. The dead fell and others jumped over their bodies. The staccato rattle of machine guns blended with the roar of exploding rocket shells, the ugly cough of napalm.

'Jesus!' said Longridge. 'Look at the damn things come!'

'They can't break,' said Easton. 'They can't turn. They can't retreat. The pressure from the rear won't let them.'

Webb said nothing. He stood with the others in the back of an adapted agricultural machine in which had been mounted a machine gun and a rocket launcher. Two other vehicles similarly armed stood to either side. The three trucks comprised his entire reserve.

It isn't enough, he thought grimly. The pressure is too great, too even. One part of the line will break and, when it does, the rest will follow. I've got a choice, he told himself. I can use all my fire-power to strengthen a selected spot or I can spread it out to bolster the line. But all I can do now is to wait and see what happens.

'Let's get at them,' said Longridge impatiently. 'What the hell are we standing here for?'

'Shut up,' said Easton. 'Webb knows what he's doing.' He looked back over the settlement. The women were in the huts with the doors open but ready to close if needed. They'll be safe enough, he thought. They've got a few guns and the logs are thick. If the worst should happen the huts will provide plenty of defence. He looked at the growing crops and felt a cold rage at the thought of their destruction. It mustn't happen, he told himself. We mustn't let it happen.

'Listen!' said Webb. His mind was busy with absorbed data, clinking like a computer as he integrated fire-power, men, targets, and supplies. This is a damn funny war, he thought. It's like fighting machines. They don't run away, give themselves up or lose their morale. They just keep coming and coming and we have to keep shooting them down. He tensed as the firing slackened at one end of the line. It resumed with added fury only to slacken again. Webb sprang up on the side of the truck, steadying himself against the rocket launcher. He could see smoke and flame and a mill of dirty green bodies. This is it, he thought, and made his decision.

'We'll spread out,' he said to the others as he jumped down from his perch. 'You know your positions. Stay back of the guard posts and give them hell. If the line should break use the truck as a strong-point. If the men should scatter give them what cover you can but get out before you get overrun. Rendezvous at the ship if things go all to hell. Now move!'

The three trucks fanned out, moving forward and firing as they went. It was like shooting into a cloud. The bullets seemed to make no difference to the bounding mass of creatures who threatened at any moment to swamp the guns with targets.

'Look at them!' The man at the machine gun hosed a hail of steel and tracer at the attackers. His eyes jerked as he tried to follow their erratic, bounding rhythm. 'God! Aren't they ever going to stop?'

Easton was too busy to answer. He fed a shell into the launcher, aimed, fired the missile. Napalm flowered, spreading flame, turning hoppers into animated fireworks. He fired again, again, working with a mechanical efficiency, laying down an arc of protective fire.

The bed of the truck shook a little. The gunner swore, readjusted his weapon, recommenced firing. The truck jerked and a deep, low rumble came from the ground. The dirt heaved, rearing up beneath the vehicle so that the machine gun fired uselessly at the sky.

'Earthquake!' The gunner clutched at the vehicle as the truck fell, jouncing on its springs. 'Let's get the hell out of here!'

'Stay where you are!' Easton fed a shell into the launcher. 'Damn you!' he yelled at the gunner. 'Stay where you are!'

The ground heaved again. The truck rose, tilted, hung sickeningly for a moment before crashing down on its side. Easton fell clear, rolling as he hit the dirt. The gunner screamed with the pain of a crushed pelvis. A silence fell along the perimeter.

'Keep firing!' Easton shouted towards the riflemen. 'For God's sake keep firing!'

He tore the pistol from his belt, aimed, fired, fired again as a shape came bounding towards him, holding back the trigger until it dropped. He rolled so that his back was hard against the truck, crouching, hugging the protection of the vehicle. Something heavy landed on the far side and the gunner stopped screaming. Something else hit the top, teetered, bounced down on its way to the river. A third hopper hit the truck and knocked it back on its wheels. It bounced, rocked, and something hard slammed against the side of Easton's head.

'This,' said Longridge feelingly, 'is one hell of a mess.' He stood beside Easton, his clothing torn, dirt on his face, his eyes wild. 'I thought you were dead,' he said. 'I spotted your truck going over. The next thing I knew the hoppers were all over us. A stampede,' he said. 'That's what it was. A damn stampede.'

'Yes,' said Easton. His throat was dry, his head ached and there was a swelling on one temple. His left leg from the knee down was numb as if something heavy had trodden on it.

'You were lucky,' said Longridge. 'An inch to the right and that wheel would have crushed your skull. The hoppers must have jumped all over you. You were lucky,' he repeated. 'A damn sight luckier than most.' His voice was high, strained. 'The screams,' he said. 'The noise. God, I never want to see anything like it again.'

'What's the position?'

'Webb's safe. He's at the perimeter seeing what he can do. If you ask me that's nothing at all. They were the first to die.'

But not the last, thought Easton. He looked over the settlement. It was unrecognizable, a churned and trampled sea of mud. The crops had vanished, the carefully measured areas completely obliterated. The huts had gone, scattered logs and planks littered the mud where they had stood. Limp figures lay beneath and beside the wreckage. Power lines trailed like forgotten pieces of string. A few dead hoppers lay sprawled in the mud which stretched down clear to the river.

'The quake did it,' said Longridge. 'We might have stood a chance but for that. The huts just came apart at the seams. Those who escaped being crushed were sitting ducks for the hoppers.' He dragged his foot in the mud. 'A few escaped,' he said. 'Not many.'

'How many?'

'We had close to ninety per cent casualties,' said the engineer. 'All dead, no wounded.' He hesitated. 'Doris was among them.'

Easton didn't comment.

'They should have been in the ship,'

234

said Longridge bitterly. 'They would have been safe there.'

Like Adrienne, thought Easton. Like Celia and Barman. Like a few more of the favoured ones. Favoured or lucky it added up to the same thing. They were alive while others were dead. But you didn't know, he told himself. You couldn't have known that the quake would hit when it did. The huts were proof against hopper attack. They had guns and could have beaten them off if some had broken through the line. They would have been safe and could even have been able to protect the crops. And we had to try and save them, he thought. We had to do that.

'Those women,' said Longridge. 'Those poor, damn women.' He kicked again at the mud. 'What do we do now?'

'Do?' Easton looked at the engineer. He hates me, he thought. He blames this on to me, all of it. Well, maybe he's right. I give the orders. I make the decisions. If anyone is to blame then it has to be me. 'There's only one thing we can do,' he said deliberately. 'We pick up the pieces.

We pick them up and we keep on going. What else?'

'We could move. With the crops gone and the buildings destroyed there's no reason now for us to stay in this place.'

'No,' admitted Easton. 'There's no reason at all.' He looked towards the north, trying to ignore the throbbing ache of his skull, eyes narrowed as he searched the horizon. Thick smoke plumed from somewhere in the mountains, darkening clouds, spreading in a sombre pall. A funeral pyre, he thought, and felt a sudden anger against the planet, the hoppers, and himself.

'Here comes Webb,' said Longridge. He sucked in his breath. 'Jesus! Is that all he could find?'

The blond giant looked a mess. His shirt hung in rags, his face was stained with dirt and smoke, a crude bandage was tied about his upper left arm. He led a small cluster of men in much the same condition. He halted before the captain.

'They knocked the hell out of us,' he said wearily. 'The only ones alive were lucky enough to be in the guard posts.

They were the only things which managed to stand up to the quake.' His eyes drifted past the captain to the devastation beyond. 'Trebor's dead,' he said. 'Trebor and a hell of a lot more. I guess that I'll have to tell his wife.'

'No,' said Longridge. 'You won't have to do that.'

'She too?'

The engineer nodded.

'That's too bad,' said Webb. 'I liked Doris. I liked her a lot.'

'We all liked her,' said Easton. He looked again towards the north. The air was thick, heavier than usual, tainted with a harsh, metallic odour. His skin prickled to primitive warnings of danger. 'What about the hoppers?' he asked Webb. 'Do you think there'll be another attack?'

'No. We might get a few stragglers but that's about all. The main body must have passed through.'

'Then we can work undefended?'

'We've got no choice,' said Webb grimly. 'If a hopper wants to pass through then we let it.' He looked curiously at the captain. 'What's on your mind?'

'Salvage. I want to collect all usable gear and stow it within the ship,' said Easton. 'The women can help stack it and they can prepare a meal at the same time. The rest will start work at once and keep on working as long as possible.'

'Leave it to me,' said Webb. He straightened a little, happier now that he had something definite to do. 'I'll detail a rifleman to each work party. I'll set up a defensive post at the base of the ship too. The women can handle that.'

'Yes,' said Easton. 'I guess they can.' He waited until Webb and his men had moved away. 'How long will it take to make the ship fully operational?' he asked Longridge.

'Not long. Why?'

'Do it,' said Easton. 'I want it ready to take off at a word.'

'Do you think we'll have to?'

'We might. Get to it.'

'Sure,' said Longridge. He looked up as a sound came from above. It was the helicopter returning from its trip to the north and it brought news.

Rodgers had found Holmson's auxiliary.

★ ★ ★

'It's way up north,' said the pilot. 'North and to the east, right on the edge of what Williams said was the volcanic zone.' He leaned forward and made an adjustment to his controls. The pitch of the rotors altered a trifle as they bit into the heavy air.

'You're sure about this?' Easton shifted in his seat, easing the straps which held him secure. 'There's no mistake?'

'I saw it,' said Rodgers. 'I actually saw the damn thing go down.' He shook his head. 'It was the queerest thing. I was circling while Williams studied the ground below. The smoke was pretty bad so I lifted to climb out of it. I turned and there it was.'

'The auxiliary?'

'That's right. Travelling like a bat out of hell. It streaked across my line of vision and then something went wrong. Turbulence, I guess. There was a lot of hot air and some tricky currents rise from mountains at the best of times.' Rodgers paused. 'Holmson wasn't a very experienced pilot,' he said quietly. 'He didn't really stand a chance.'

'If it was Holmson.'

'It was him right enough,' said the pilot. 'I recognized the auxiliary. Hell,' he said. 'I rode down here in its twin. That auxiliary is back with the ship. Who else but Holmson would have one exactly like it?'

Easton didn't answer. He relaxed in his seat, glad of the chance to rest, the opportunity to ease his aching head. Below him the terrain moved steadily past. It was convoluted, torn, scarred with gashes of naked dirt, the vegetation ripped away to reveal the stony ground. The quake, he told himself. The tremors must have run from the river right back up here. Or from up here right down to the river.

'What's it like up in the mountains?' he asked. 'What did Williams have to say?' There had been no time to talk with the geologist but Rodgers would know.

'Bad,' said the pilot. 'He reckons that the entire area is in the process of geologic upheaval. We spotted some volcanic craters that were obviously very old and some others, still old but showing smoke.'

'The smoke we can see now?'

'No. That comes from deeper in the range. Williams guessed that new volcanoes were in the process of formation. He said that conditions were right for the entire mass to burst in eruption.' He leaned forward and made more adjustments to his controls. 'I'm trying to conserve fuel,' he explained. 'We didn't get the chance to refuel back at the settlement.'

'No,' said Easton. The fuel had gone with almost everything else.

'It looked like hell back there,' said Rodgers. 'Sheer hell.'

'It was.' Easton craned forward as something dark rose towards them. A cloud of ash spotted the cabin with ebony snowflakes, swirling as the blast of the rotors churned the air. 'Is it much further?'

'No.' Rodgers swore as more ash occluded his vision. 'This damn stuff makes it hard to see,' he complained. The helicopter rose and droned towards the northeast. 'It's by an outcrop of reddish stone. There's a little stream to the south and a crevass to the northwest.' He hung his head from the cabin and grunted. 'Got it. Stand by for landing.'

The helicopter bumped, settled, came to rest. Rodgers cut the engine and looked at Easton. The captain was checking his pistol.

'You won't need that,' said Rodgers.

'You've forgotten something.' Easton rammed back the magazine and operated the slide. 'Just because that is our auxiliary it doesn't follow that Holmson must be inside it. He saw something, remember? Maybe he crashed and who-ever it was he saw managed to repair and fly it.'

'You won't need that,' said Rodgers again. 'Come and see.'

★　★　★

The auxiliary was a mess, the wings torn from the body, the tail assembly a complete ruin. The hull itself was split for two-thirds of its length, the nose driven back into the cabin, the retrojets clogged with rock and dirt. Easton stared at it, looked down the path which it must have taken, stared at the wreck again.

'It hit hard,' said Rodgers. 'Convection currents, I guess, like I told you. They must have torn it from control and sent it smack into the ground. You won't need that gun,' he added. 'I told you that. There's nothing living inside.'

'You're sure about that?'

'I'm sure.'

Holmson was dead but, by some freak of the crash, his body had not been mangled. He was still strapped in his seat, head lolling on his shoulders, mouth and chest stained with blood from his punctured lungs. His eyes were open. Gently Easton closed them then looked at Rodgers. 'You knew,' he said. 'You knew all the time.'

'Yes,' admitted the pilot. 'I landed when I found it. I saw what was inside.'

'Why didn't you tell me?'

'Would you have believed it?' Rodgers shook his head. 'Hell, I don't believe it myself. Where has he been all this time? Why didn't he contact us? Did he crash somewhere and manage to effect his own repairs? Did he find someone to do them for him?'

Easton didn't answer.

'I could find out about that,' said Rodgers. 'But I need time and equipment to do it. I'd have to pull everything apart,' he explained. 'Check every item piece by piece. It could have been a defective wire,' he pointed out. 'Something as small as that.' He glowered at the wrecked cabin. 'Or maybe it wasn't that at all,' he suggested. 'He could have been held a prisoner somewhere and only now managed to escape. Or maybe he didn't escape. Maybe they just let him go.'

'Yes,' said Easton. He reached forward and touched the dead man gently on the cheek, running his fingers down over the flesh and beneath the jaw.

'No beard,' said Rodgers. 'I noticed that. Perhaps he managed to shave too?'

'Perhaps,' said Easton. He stooped and looked at the dead man's shoes, lifting each foot in turn and examining soles and heels. He turned up the collar of the tunic, felt in the pockets, finally lifted the lips and examined the teeth. He was frowning as he straightened and looked around the cabin. The radio had burst from its housing. He checked it and found the switch turned to the 'on' position.

'He's dead,' said Rodgers. 'That's the only thing we can be sure about. The poor devil,' he added. 'He came so close to making it.'

Outside the sky had darkened and a thin rain of dirty black ash drifted from the clouds to settle as a gritty film. The metallic odour had increased so that it was now a literal taste in the mouth. Rodgers led the way towards his machine. 'We'd better get out of here,' he said. 'Quick, before something breaks.'

He took off with a roar from the engine, the whirling rotors churning the ash-filled air, biting deep as they hauled the cabin up and away. It was like flying through a blizzard, thought Easton. A snowstorm of black flakes instead of white. The ash clung to the windows and piled high in the cabin.

'Williams said that something like this might happen,' said Rodgers. 'One of those damn mountains is getting ready to blow its top. Let's hope that we can get far enough away before it does.'

Easton nodded, looking towards the north. The thick plume of smoke had grown to a towering column of darkness, twisting and spreading as it rose so that it seemed to threaten the entire sky. Even as he watched a red glow shone from its base and a shower of sparks sprayed upwards and then down. The helicopter jerked in a sudden turbulence.

'Damn,' said Rodgers. 'Damn and hell to the lousy luck!'

'Something wrong?'

'We're not going to make it,' said the pilot. 'It's taking too much power to claw our way through this soup and we haven't got the fuel. Start dumping,' he ordered. 'Throw out everything we don't need.'

It wasn't much. The cushions, the

seats, the safety straps. Easton tore out the radio and threw it outside. The flares went next, the emergency survival kit, the tools.

'Hang on,' said Rodgers. He fed power to the rotors and let them pull the cabin higher, higher, so high that they left the ash behind and Easton could see the base of the column of smoke, the raw, red fury of seething fires striving to escape. 'We might just be lucky,' said the pilot. 'With a strong tail wind we might just about make it back to the ship.'

'If not?'

'We walk.'

They walked. The helicopter crashed a mile from their destination and they walked. Slowly. Rodgers had twisted his foot and leaned heavily on Easton's shoulder.

'We'll make it,' said the captain. 'All we have to do is to just keep going.'

'Sure,' said Rodgers. 'That's all.'

'The hoppers have gone,' said Easton. 'We don't have to worry about them.'

'I'm not,' said Rodgers. He hopped along, his face contorted with pain. 'It's that mountain,' he said. 'You saw it. It's liable to go off at any moment. When it does it'll spew red hot lava from here to the middle of next week. If — ' He broke off as the ground shook. 'Down!' he screamed. 'Quick!'

The concussion wave hit as they clutched the dirt. Trees flattened before a blast of hot wind which stank of sulphur and metal. Debris smashed down around them, hot, smoking lumps of rock and stone. Fires sprang from where they rested against living wood.

'Come on!' Easton rose to his feet, pulling the pilot up after him. 'Come on!' he yelled as the man staggered. 'Move!'

'I can't!' Rodgers hopped, stumbled, almost fell. 'I can't,' he yelled again. 'The damn foot won't take my weight!'

Easton looked behind him, to the north where the smoke had spread to a giant fan and where flaming masses of molten rock sprayed like water from a fountain. Even as he looked a second explosion ripped the air, numbing his ears, snatching the breath from his lungs.

'Come on!' He stooped, flung the pilot

over his shoulders and ran from the bursting mountain. The ship had been at least a mile from where they had crashed. They had covered some distance. How long would it take him to cover the rest?

He could feel the heat as he came in sight of the perimeter, the hot, dry, searing heat which signalled the advance of the sea of molten rock pouring from the mountain, the burning stuff running like water. A third explosion ripped the air as he passed the clogged rifle pits, the concussion throwing him down, filling the air with flaming debris as the volcano roared in the agony of its birth.

The ground shook in sympathy, quivering, fissures gaping as internal stresses fought for equilibrium.

'Leave me,' said Rodgers. He tried to stand, to take a step. 'Leave me,' he repeated. 'You damned, stupid fool! Leave me!'

'Shut up!' Easton fought for breath, using precious moments as he inflated his chest, oxygenating his blood. 'We're almost there.'

The ground shook again as he lifted the pilot back onto his shoulders. Grimly he raced towards the ship. The lower entry port was open but there was no sign of life. Everyone would be inside the vessel by now. Inside and, he hoped, strapped down.

He stumbled and almost fell, the weight on his shoulders driving him towards the mud. Muscles cried in protest as he regained his balance and forged onwards. Before him the ship trembled, swaying, the nose tracing an arc across the sky. He felt panic grip his stomach, weakening his legs so that he seemed to run as if in a nightmare. The ship swayed again, slowly, gracefully, like a tree about to fall. He ran even faster, flinging himself across the mud, ignoring the searing agony of his lungs.

Then he was at the port, throwing Rodgers from his shoulders, falling through the opening to slam the door and croak orders with the last of his breath.

'Blast!' he panted. 'Take off! Now!'

He heard the thunder of the rockets, felt pressure, saw the metal floor come up and hit him as invisible weight pressed him down.

12

'You were lucky,' said Barman. 'Three times lucky to be exact.' He adjusted a hypogun and fired it at Easton's arm. 'Antibiotics,' he explained. 'They help.'

'Yes,' said Easton. 'I suppose they do.' He looked around. As far as he could see he was the only occupant of the tiny hospital. 'I passed out,' he said. 'In the entry port. Right?'

Barman nodded. 'As I was saying,' he continued. 'You were lucky. Another minute and you'd have had the backside roasted from your bones and that's no exaggeration. You've got quite a few third degree burns. The second thing is that if you'd hung about much longer the ship would have taken off without you. We had it set on emergency control,' he explained. 'If — the degree of tilt had passed the safety figure the pilot would have taken off. Longridge fixed that up,' he said. 'He and Adrienne.'

'They would,' said Easton. He remembered the terror he had felt at the sight of the swaying vessel. All for nothing, really. 'But you can't be certain that the ship would have passed the safety margin,' he pointed out.

'True,' admitted the biomech. 'But I think it very likely.'

'What was the third thing?'

'For that you can thank the pilot. It threw the ship into M-space right away. As soon as the fins left dirt. That reduced the acceleration pressure and undoubtedly saved your life.'

'I can stand high-G,' reminded Easton.

'Sure you can,' agreed the biomech. 'You're a strong, healthy cuss with hair on your chest and we all know that you can take it. But you'd just run almost a mile over rough ground at top speed and with a fully grown man riding on your shoulders. You'd also been breathing air loaded with ash, sulphur and other assorted filth. Your blood was crying out for oxygen and your lungs were having a hell of a fight to get it.'

'So?'

252

'Normally a man will fall unconscious when in such a state. Sometimes they die but not often, not when the heart is in good condition. But you were in a ship which had just taken off. The strain was tremendous. If you had been subjected to the full, normal acceleration pressure what do you think would have happened to you? You would have died,' said Barman. 'No doubt about it. You simply wouldn't have had the strength to suck air into your lungs. As it was,' he said casually, 'I had the devil of a time feeding you pressurized oxygen.'

'Thank you,' said Easton. 'I'm glad you took the trouble.' He tried to sit upright but couldn't. Restraints held him fast to the couch. A drip flask was connected to one arm by a length of plastic tubing. Saline, he guessed, and probably glucose too. I must have been in a bad way, he thought. But I'm no athlete. Strong, perhaps, but that's all. It isn't the same. He remembered the pilot. 'Rodgers?'

'He's all right,' said Barman. 'He was the one who did the riding. I've fixed up his ankle and he's as good as new. Do you want to see him?'

'Not yet.' Easton lay back, thinking. 'What's happening?' he demanded. 'Where are we heading?'

'Nowhere.' Barman picked up the hypogun and made a careful adjustment. Casually he aimed it at the side of Easton's throat. 'We're orbiting Eden,' he said. 'We're going to keep orbiting until we've cleaned up the ship. I want to sterilize every molecule of air,' he explained. 'Every atom of material. There's one thing from that planet I don't want to carry with us.'

The birth-destructive virus, thought Easton. Barman would naturally think of that. 'And after?'

'Then we have to decide,' said the biomech. 'What to do and where to go.'

'All of us?'

'That's right,' said Barman. He touched the release of the hypogun. Air and drugs blasted at the captain's throat. 'Dope,' said Barman. 'To make you sleep. You need rest,' he explained. 'A lot of it.'

'Barman!'

'What is it?'

'I'm still the captain,' reminded Easton drowsily. 'I'm still in command.'

'Yes,' said Barman. 'We know that.'

* * *

The control room was very quiet and only the light from the tell-tales, the shimmering greyness of the screens illuminated the compartment. Against the light of the screens Easton was a vague silhouette. He turned as the door opened and Adrienne entered the room. 'They've decided?'

'Yes.'

'To return?'

'Yes,' she said again. 'They want to go home. The cowards,' she added. 'The cowards!'

'Why? Because they recognize defeat when they see it?' He leaned forward and touched a switch. Light bloomed from hidden sources. 'Don't blame them,' he told the girl. 'I gave them the right to decide for themselves.'

'Rodgers tried,' she said. 'I think he would follow you to hell if you asked. Longridge too, he was loyal. Webb even, but hardly anyone else. The majority vote is that you proceed at once to Earth. They asked me to tell you,' she said. 'I wish they hadn't.'

He rose and stood facing her.

'They've all been too damned civilized about it,' she said furiously. 'They've waited until you were well and able to take full charge of the ship. Until you were able to talk to them. But you didn't,' she accused. 'You left it all to them.'

'That's democracy,' he reminded.

'So they said. They think a lot of you — but only a handful voted for you.'

'Which way did you vote, Adrienne?'

'Need you ask? She looked up at him, her eyes large in the translucent whiteness of her face. 'I voted to stand by anything you decided,' she said. 'Anything at all.'

'Good,' he said. 'Then no one is going to be disappointed.' He turned from her and looked at the screens. 'We're on our way,' he said. 'We've been on our way since Barman gave the ship a clean bill of health. We're going home.'

'To Earth?'

'Home,' he repeated.

'But why? I thought — ' She broke off, confused.

'You thought that I'd go anywhere, do anything, just so long as I could be the big fish in the small pond. Is that it? Well,' he said, 'maybe that was true, once. It isn't any longer. I've seen too many die for that. I've lost too many good friends. I don't want to lose any more.'

'You're going back to trouble,' she reminded. 'You know that?'

'There'll be no trouble.'

'Perhaps not.' She frowned, thinking. 'This is the only ship of its kind,' she mused. 'The only one with the hidrive. That must be worth something. They'll forgive a lot if we take it back to them. They may even let you go out again,' she said. 'Let us go out again. There are other planets we could try. Hundreds of them.'

He shook his head.

'They will,' she insisted. 'They must. If they hope to get the ship they'll have to.'

'You don't understand. Listen,' he said. 'Eden was about the most promising world we could have found. It had everything — but we couldn't live on it.

257

Can you guess why?'

She stood, waiting.

'How long has man been on Earth? Two million years? At least that,' he said. 'Two million years of mutation and adaption and we still haven't conquered our environment. We still suffer from disease. There are still certain foods we cannot eat. How long do you think it would take for a race to become acclimatized to an alien world?'

'I don't know,' she said. 'And I don't care. To me you seem to be finding an excuse for failure.'

'That's right,' he admitted. 'I failed. That's all there is to it.'

You're wrong, she thought. So wrong. You didn't fail. You made mistakes, she admitted, but you were forced into making them. With a different type of personnel things could have been different. We're not the pioneers we thought we were, she told herself. We wanted to take too much with us. The comforts and luxuries we had left behind. We were scared and frightened when we should have been courageous and bold. Did the real pioneers act like that? Did they wait to see that every risk had been eliminated? Did they put their trust in rats?

We tried to find something, she thought bleakly. And now it's too late.

'Don't blame yourself, David,' she said. 'Please don't do that.'

'I won't,' he said and reached for her. 'Perhaps it was a lesson we had to learn. Perhaps a lot of things but I'm only concerned now with one. Do you remember here in this room with dead men lying on the floor? You remember what you said?'

'I love you, David, and I know that you love me. From now on everything is going to be wonderful!'

'Do you still think that?'

'Yes,' she said. 'Oh, yes.'

'Even on Earth?'

'Anywhere,' she said. 'Anywhere at all.'

★   ★   ★

There was something wrong with Earth. It swam beneath them, a mottled ball of bluish-white splotched with brown and blue and dusty green. To one side rode the moon, the scarred face unmistakable but . . .

'Try again,' said Rodgers. 'Keep on trying. Damn it,' he said plaintively, 'the whole planet can't be under radio silence. It doesn't make sense. Are you sure that your equipment is in working order?'

'Yes,' snapped Longridge. He was as baffled as the pilot and getting just as annoyed. 'The ether is dead,' he insisted. 'Stone, cold dead. Not a peep of any kind. Not a squeak on the entire band. I've tried them all. It's just like Eden — nothing.'

'Maybe it's happened?' suggested Celia. She moved a little closer to her husband. 'We expected it,' she reminded. 'That was the reason for building the ship. We've been away a long time, maybe longer than we know. Perhaps the entire planet is dead.'

'No,' said Barman quickly. His hand closed comfortingly on Celia's. 'That can't be true. There's vegetation,' he pointed out. 'Radioactivity kills everything. Fish, fowl, animals and insects and plants. The lot.'

'The vegetation could have grown back,' suggested Webb. 'Maybe the radiation wasn't as strong as we thought or maybe — ' He broke off, looking at Adrienne. She felt his eyes.

'Yes?'

'Maybe this isn't Earth at all,' he blurted. 'Maybe the pilot made a mistake. There has to be some reason,' he insisted. 'If that's the Earth it should be either inhabited or dead. If inhabited we should be able to pick up radio signals all over the band. Damn it, we had a civilization that covered the planet! If what we were afraid of has happened then why all the vegetation? So it can't be the Earth. There's been some mistake.'

Adrienne looked at him then at Easton. He sat, adding nothing to the discussion, relaxed as if unsurprised. 'There's been no mistake,' he said.

'There has to be,' said Webb.

'Let's make sure.' Barman stepped to the controls. 'Ship to pilot,' he said to the instruments. 'Is the planet we are orbiting the planet Earth?'

'It is.'

'Are you certain?'

'There is no possibility of error,' said the mechanical voice coldly. 'I have checked on the other satellites of this system.'

'And the sun? Have you checked on that?'

'I have.'

'I don't get it,' said Barman. He was puzzled. 'The pilot seems to know what it's talking about.' He frowned at the screens, the stars depicted on their surfaces. 'The constellations look about right,' he murmured. 'I'm no astronomer but they look as they should. At least,' he added, 'they look as I remember them. And the moon seems normal enough. But where are the space stations? Where is Lunar Base?'

'There should be cities,' said Webb. He increased the magnification of one of the screens. 'Even if there are no people the cities would still be there and we should be able to see them. London covered well over a hundred square miles. It should stand out like a sore thumb.' He looked at Barman. 'Try the pilot again.'

'I have. There's no point in repeating

what we already know.'

'I'll do it,' said Adrienne. She sat at the controls. 'Ship to pilot. Is this the planet Earth?'

'It is.'

'The same planet we left when we began our journey?'

The pilot didn't answer. Adrienne repeated the question.

'Yes,' said the pilot. 'And no. It depends on the precise meaning of your question.'

'The thing's gone crazy,' said Barman in disgust. 'It wants to play games.'

'No,' said Easton. He rose to his feet. 'The pilot is making perfect sense,' he said. 'This is Earth, yes. But it is not the same planet we left. Not exactly. This is the Earth as it was a long time ago. A very long time.'

He looked at their faces.

'Yes,' he said. 'That's right. We've travelled backwards in time.'

* * *

'You should have guessed,' he said to Rodgers. 'You had all the evidence. It was

263

right in front of you. We saw it together.'

'Holmson?' The pilot looked startled. 'Is that what you mean?'

Easton nodded. 'He left the ship,' he said. 'He dropped down to Eden. He saw something incredible. So incredible that he couldn't believe it. Then the ship engaged the hi-drive and we lost contact.'

'He crashed,' said Rodgers. 'He must have done.'

'He crashed, yes, in fact you saw him do it,' said Easton. 'You were probably the cause. He'd seen the ship,' he explained. 'He'd seen the clearing but the one thing which really threw him was in seeing you. The rest was startling but when he saw the helicopter and saw you looking at him through the cabin it was too much. He couldn't accept the possibility of what he saw. He was disorganized, lost control and the convection currents threw him into the ground.'

'No,' said Rodgers. 'No.'

'It has to be that way,' said Easton. 'He hadn't crashed when the ship moved into hi-drive. He was startled but that was all. He crashed later when he saw you in the helicopter.' He saw Rodgers' disbelieving expressionn. 'Damn it, man,' he snapped, 'think about it. Holmson was clean shaven — where did he get a razor? His teeth were clean — how? He carried no food or spare clothing and yet he was in prime condition and the soles of his shoes weren't even marked by dust. He looked exactly as he did when he took down the auxiliary. That was six months before we found him. Are you trying to say that he lived on Eden all that time, without food, without spare clothing, without a razor or toothpaste, soap, brush or comb? Lived on the land, managed to repair his auxiliary and still, somehow, managed to look as he did when we found him?'

'I guess not,' said Rodgers slowly. 'But how could he have been thrown back in time?'

'He wasn't,' said Easton. 'We were.'

'The hi-drive,' said Adrienne. 'When we lost contact with Holmson. The ship entered M-space and — '

'We travelled back through time,' interrupted Easton. 'About six months back to be exact. It has to be that way,' he pointed out. 'There is no other logical explanation. It is the only way we can account for what happened to Holmson. I guessed what must have happened then. This,' he gestured to the screens, 'proves it.'

'Wait a minute,' said Barman. He scowled as he thought about it. 'There's something you've left out,' he complained. 'The ship jerked back while we were orbiting Eden. While Holmson was in the auxiliary. Why did it do that?'

Easton looked at Adrienne. 'Tell him.'

'I don't know,' she confessed. 'The pilot told us that it had engaged the hi-drive to avoid danger. It said that an object of tremendous mass was approaching on a collision path. It — ' She broke off, eyes bright with understanding. 'Of course!' she said. 'It had to be that!'

'Be what?' Barman was impatient.

'The object which the pilot had to avoid was us,' said Easton. He looked at the biomech. 'You told me that when we took off the pilot immediately engaged the hi-drive. It threw the ship into M-space as soon as the fins left the ground. God knows what that did to the planet but we know what it did to us. It threw us back in time,' he explained. 'We were already retrogressing as we climbed up through the atmosphere. Climbing up on a path which would have driven us smack into ourselves as we orbited the planet. No wonder the pilot took evasion action! It must have sensed what was going to happen.'

'Wait a minute,' objected Barman. 'What you're really saying is that, at that particular point in time, we existed in two places at once. I find that a little hard to swallow.'

'Then don't try it,' advised Easton. 'It happened, that's all you need think about. One day, when you get a lot of spare time, you might like to work out the paradox. I don't intend to bother.'

'But supposing we had met ourselves?' said Barman. 'What then?'

'If we had you'd remember it,' said Easton patiently. 'As we didn't — the possibility remains unimportant. We didn't meet ourselves — so forget it.' He called to Webb who stood beside the screen with

the increased magnification. 'You were looking for London. Did you find it?'

'No.'

'You won't,' said Easton. 'But you may
find something else. A land bridge from
England to the Continent. We know that
it was there once and, if we've travelled
far enough back, it could be there now.
See if you can find it.' Webb did.

★　★　★

'Home,' said Adrienne. She stood beside
Easton in the control room. They were
alone. 'It's odd,' she said, looking at the
screen and the planet below. 'That's the
Earth but, in many ways, it's as strange as
Eden.'

'No,' he said. 'It can never be that. Two
million years,' he reminded. 'Remember?
That's how long you've been getting used
to what's below.'

'I suppose so,' she said. 'But I wasn't
thinking of that. I was thinking of what
we'd got used to. The cities and transport
and all the rest of it.' She shook her head.
'I must be just a city girl at heart. Will we

build cities, David?'

He didn't answer.

'Michele didn't know what he'd discovered,' she mused. 'He thought that he'd invented a means of travelling faster than light and that was all. Instead he'd found a means of travelling in time as well as in space. Perhaps, if he were here with us, he might be able to figure out some way of reversing the effect. Of adapting the drive in some way so that we could travel back to our own time.' She sighed, a little wistfully, and Easton looked sharply at her.

'Is that what you want?' he asked. 'To get back from where we came?'

'No,' she said. 'Not really. I was just thinking of Michele. But he isn't here.'

No, he thought, and neither is Geldray and Dolman, Doris and Trebor and a hell of a lot of other people who had as much right to live as any of us. But they're dead, he told himself. Rotting on some alien planet or killed by our blast. But they're not even born yet. None of them is. Perhaps none of them will ever be. Perhaps none of us here will be born either. But that's stupid, he told himself. I'm alive, standing here and thinking about it and that means — what?

Perhaps history isn't what we've always thought it was, he mused. Perhaps it isn't a single line from beginning to end, something fixed and immutable. Maybe we're being given a second chance. This Earth below is the same but now, perhaps, we can make it into something different from the one we knew. We have knowledge, he told himself. We have skills and can draw on the lessons of the past. We don't have to make the same mistakes. We don't have to follow the same, old, destructive path. We know where that leads now, he thought. This time it could be different.

'We can live down there,' said Adrienne. 'We know that. We can build and harvest, grow and plan. And we can have children,' she said softly. 'Children that will grow strong and tall. This is our world,' she said proudly. 'Home.'

'Home,' he agreed and repeated the word. 'Home.'

It had a wonderful sound.

We do hope that you have enjoyed reading this large print book.

Did you know that all of our titles are available for purchase?

We publish a wide range of high quality large print books including:
Romances, Mysteries, Classics
General Fiction
Non Fiction and Westerns

Special interest titles available in large print are:
The Little Oxford Dictionary
Music Book, Song Book
Hymn Book, Service Book

Also available from us courtesy of Oxford University Press:
Young Readers' Dictionary
(large print edition)
Young Readers' Thesaurus
(large print edition)

For further information or a free brochure, please contact us at:
Ulverscroft Large Print Books Ltd.,
The Green, Bradgate Road, Anstey,
Leicester, LE7 7FU, England.
Tel: (00 44) **0116 236 4325**
Fax: (00 44) **0116 234 0205**

Other titles in the
Linford Mystery Library:

THE GREEN HELIX

E. C. Tubb

Spaceships, including the *Jason*, the *Starbird* and the *Invincible*, had disappeared into hyperspace — never to return. Everyone assumed that their disappearances were due to mechanical failure. But then the *Invincible* was found deserted, drifting in space, six months after vanishing. The ship's engines were undamaged, the hull intact — but there was no sign of life aboard — no trace of its crew or the two hundred passengers. What had happened? Was it something or *somebody* out there in hyperspace?